From the desk of
Jeffrey Addams Logan III

*Spot-check the new hotel

*Meet with the staff

*Lunch with Father—talk about the future

*Buy books on pregnancy

*Learn how to diaper a baby

*Think of baby names

*Practice calling myself "Daddy"

ABOUT THE AUTHOR

Mollie Molay started writing years ago when, as a going-away present, her co-workers gave her an electric typewriter. Since then, she's gone on to become president of the Los Angeles Romance Writers of America. A part-time travel agent, Mollie loves to travel, and spends whatever spare time she has volunteering; she's grateful for her good fortune and wants to give back to those around her. She lives in California.

Books by Mollie Molay

HARLEQUIN AMERICAN ROMANCE

Don't miss any of our special offers. Write to us at the following address for information on our newest releases.

Harlequin Reader Service
U.S.: 3010 Walden Ave., P.O. Box 1325, Buffalo, NY 14269
Canadian: P.O. Box 609, Fort Erie, Ont. L2A 5X3

Father In
Training

MOLLIE MOLAY

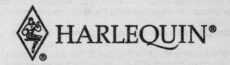

HARLEQUIN®

TORONTO • NEW YORK • LONDON
AMSTERDAM • PARIS • SYDNEY • HAMBURG
STOCKHOLM • ATHENS • TOKYO • MILAN • MADRID
PRAGUE • WARSAW • BUDAPEST • AUCKLAND

My thanks to Joan Engberg, my partner in travel
and in writing, for her help in the final editing of
the completed manuscript.
And to critique groups everywhere, especially mine.
Betty Moss, Aline Thompson, Linga Guss, Ann Finnin,
RisaLee Miller and Joan, I thank you.

ISBN 0-373-16776-8

FATHER IN TRAINING

Weekly Astrological Forecast

Los Angeles Gazette

Aries

Your wishes are fulfilled in a rapid manner. Scenario features romance, style, creativity, prosperity. Are you ready for love and marriage? Cancer native plays exciting role.

Chapter One

Moonlight became her.

Jeffrey Logan sauntered onto the lush patio of Acapulco's Concordia Hotel to catch a closer glimpse of the woman he'd noticed that morning on the white sandy beach.

The blue-white glow of moonlight caressed the curves of her slender body. She was dressed in a short black wisp of a cocktail dress that was no more than a slip. Bare at the shoulders, the dress was held up with straps so slender as to be almost invisible. Whoever she was, she attracted more than one envious look from passing female guests, and admiring glances from their escorts.

Earlier in the day, she'd worn a one-piece bathing suit that fit her trim figure like a second skin. Her long, blond hair had been drawn away from her face and twisted into a chignon at the nape of her neck. The silken tresses framed finely honed cheekbones, porcelain skin and eyes the blue-green color of the glistening waters of Acapulco Bay.

Caught by an instant attraction, for a long moment

he'd wondered who she was. For another long moment he'd toyed with the idea of taking a chance and going over to introduce himself. Too late. After a deep sigh and a glance at her wristwatch, she'd gathered her belongings and disappeared into the hotel.

In sunshine or moonlight, she was a mixture of all the women he'd ever been attracted to rolled into one petite, intriguing figure.

The melodious sound of violins and guitars drifted from the bar behind him—a soft, sweet melody that spoke of hunger for a lost love. He sipped his margarita, tasted the heady combination of tequila, salt and lime. Stirred by the music, and maybe by the glow of the moon, he abruptly set his drink aside and started toward her. Tonight, he wasn't going to waste time wondering who his golden lady was and chance losing her again.

Just as he stepped forward, a man who had been loitering nearby walked up to her and held out his hand.

"Señora, you will do me the honor of sharing this dance with me, no?"

"I'm sorry," his vision said, and took a step backward, "but I can't." She glanced around apprehensively. "I—I'm waiting for someone. He should be here at any moment."

"Nonsense," the man answered. "A lovely woman such as you need not wait for any man." He took her by the elbow and started to lead her back to the hotel dining room. "Come, let us dance."

From the expression on the woman's face, Jeffrey sensed she was uneasy with the situation—maybe even frightened. With a quick look around to make sure his blond goddess was indeed alone, he strode over to the pair and held out his arms. "Sweetheart, I'm sorry I kept you waiting. I had to answer an urgent long-distance telephone call. Now that that's taken care of, I'm ready for the dance you promised me."

A brief flicker of uncertainty crossed her face, then passed as quickly as it had been born.

"No problem, honey," she said with a brilliant smile. She pulled away from her would-be dance partner and came into Jeffrey's arms. "I was just enjoying the beautiful gardens while I waited for you."

Jeffrey eyed the intruder over her head. "Señor?"

Disappointment covered the other man's face. He bowed. "My pardon, Señora. Perhaps another time." With a cool smile, he bowed and walked away.

She looked up at Jeff, relief on her face. "I don't know how to thank you," she murmured. He could feel her body tremble. "Maybe I was being foolish, but there was something about that man..."

"Don't waste your time thinking about him. He's history," Jeffrey answered. "Come on. As long as we've gotten this far, let's go inside and dance and forget everything but the music." He took one of her hands in his and drew her to the French doors leading to the dance floor where couples swayed in close embrace to a waltz.

"By the way," he said with a smile as he swung with her in his arms onto the dance floor, "I suppose I should introduce myself." Jeffrey stopped himself. He was so drawn in by this woman, so besotted by her very being, that he'd almost made a big mistake. *Be careful,* he reminded himself. *Stay low.* "I'm Logan Addams," he said finally, and with an undetectable hesitation. "And you?"

"Scarlett," she answered. A dimple danced across her cheek.

"As in O'Hara?" he teased, resisting the urge to caress the soft porcelain skin of her cheek where the dimple had come to rest.

"No, as in O'Malley." She glanced up at him under raised eyebrows. Her smile dared him to question her.

Under that smile, he could tell the lady was understandably cautious and was giving him a fictitious name. After seeing the brief encounter with the stranger who had asked her to dance, Jeffrey didn't blame her. For that matter, she didn't know Jeffrey, either. But given her seeming consent to become acquainted, that was a state he was eager to change.

Gazing into the smile that lingered on her lips, Jeffrey thought the better of explaining to her that, after all, she was a single woman in a posh tourist hotel in a foreign country. A setting where local social customs might make it okay for a man to approach a lovely woman and ask for a dance. He'd been about to do it himself. Luckily for him, she seemed to welcome his intrusion.

"This is the first time I realized a knight in shining armor could show up wearing a white dinner jacket," he heard her murmur.

"Don't fool yourself, Scarlett," he answered dryly. "I'm no hero. Not even a gallant knight in shining armor. I'm a flesh-and-blood man who happened to be in the right place at the right time."

"Maybe so, but you came to my rescue just the same."

"Yes, but it was more than that," he replied. He held her closer, and slowly revolved to the melodious strains of the violins and guitars. He muttered a silent prayer of thanks that the music was a waltz. This way, he could hold her close enough to savor her sweet scent.

"When I came out onto the terrace, I confess I was feeling kind of blue and lonely," he went on. "Everything changed when I looked up and saw you standing there in the moonlight. Something told me you were about to become a special woman in my life. You looked so lovely, I would have asked you to dance under any circumstances."

It was true, he thought when he saw her blush. He'd come to Mexico to find himself, to resolve inner conflicts and to decide on his future. A glimpse of her had changed all that. Now, all he could think of was the woman he held in his arms.

"There's a beautiful moon tonight, isn't there?"

he asked to cover her charming embarrassment. *But not half as beautiful as you are.*

"Yes, it is," she answered, gazing up over his shoulder at the new moon that hung low on the horizon. A sparkling star was so close to the curve of the moon that it appeared to hang from its tip. "You know," she added with a light laugh, "it may be the same moon that's shining at home, but somehow it looks different down here. The man in the moon is so clear, it's as if an artist painted it." A rueful grin came over her face as their eyes met. "I'm usually not so fanciful, but…"

"…the magic of moonlight can turn the most practical of people into poets," he finished for her as her voice trailed off. "And sometimes even prompts them to do things they normally wouldn't do. Like this."

For a moment, Jeffrey was tempted to show her with a kiss how pleased he was with finding that she was not only beautiful but had the soul of a poet. Instead, he held her closer to him while they circled the ballroom. "By the way, did you know that new moons are supposed to bring good luck?"

"No, I hadn't heard that old wives' tale, but it's a nice thought." She returned his smile with one that stoked the spark of desire building inside him. For a moment, she actually looked embarrassed. "As a matter of fact, I usually don't share my thoughts, and certainly not with strangers. And definitely not about something as romantic as moonlight."

"Blame it on the moon," he said, gently caressing the warm skin of her shoulders and the nape of her neck. Silk, he thought. Rare and fragile silk. "Moonlight has a way of working magic—especially the moonlight of new moons."

Her flesh was as soft as a rose petal, her scent as heady as a fine wine, he mused as he smiled down into sparkling eyes that reminded him of sunlight shining on Acapulco Bay's clear waters. "Pardon me for asking, but are you sure your name is Scarlett?"

"Yes," she said firmly. "Why do you ask?"

He shrugged. A name like Scarlett O'Malley, if true, was unusual. But then, she didn't know him, or that he hadn't given her his real name, either. Maybe she had something to hide, too. He glanced down at her shining golden hair and smiled at the thought. She might be hiding her true identity, but it made her appear mysterious and somehow even more desirable.

"Are you here alone?"

"Yes and no," she answered. "That is, my sister is with me, but she's up in our room packing."

"Packing?"

"Yes. We're leaving tomorrow."

Jeffrey felt a twinge of regret. Just his luck—he'd found the woman of his dreams, too late. But at least there was still the rest of the night to look forward to. "Forgive me if I'm being personal, but you looked so pensive out on the terrace a few minutes ago. Is something wrong?"

"Not really." She rested her head against his chest, her sigh warm against his chin. "I was just thinking about having to go home tomorrow."

"And you aren't ready to go back?" he asked. Maybe he could persuade her to stay another few days. At least long enough to find out where she lived so he could find her again.

"I'm afraid not." She gestured to the lush, tropical growth surrounding the hotel patio, where palm trees waved under a gentle evening breeze and tropical flowers scented the warm air. Like thousands of stars, the city lights that rimmed Acapulco Bay turned the horizon into a fairyland. "A week surrounded by all of this loveliness hasn't been long enough," she added wistfully.

"But you're here now." Impulsively, Jeffrey reached to finger the few golden strands of her hair that had managed to escape the confines of diamond pins—pins that resembled captured stars. Their hands brushed as they simultaneously reached to push the hair out of her eyes. Rather than being turned off by their brief contact, she gave him a shy smile that encouraged him to take a step that was totally unlike him. "How would you like to take a walk around the hotel grounds with me?"

He waited with baited breath for her answer.

SURPRISED AT HER unexpected and instant response to his invitation, Abby Carson glanced up at the new moon. He was right—moonlight *had* cast a spell on her. Why else was she experiencing half-forgotten pleasurable sensations, let alone looking forward to spending the rest of the evening in his company? A man she'd never met until an hour ago and would probably never meet again?

Their meeting hadn't been one she'd planned, she thought. Nor expected. And certainly not at this stage of her life. Lately, dating had become more of a chore than a pleasure, her choices narrowed by the odds that as she grew older she had less of a chance to meet an eligible man her own age.

She hadn't been completely honest with Mr. Addams, either. Before the other stranger had asked her to dance, her thoughts had been more on an awareness of a major milestone in her life—her fortieth birthday—not on home. She'd been reflecting on how quickly her life was passing—and how many dreams were still unfulfilled.

Now her thoughts were happily on this man, this Logan Addams who had appeared out of nowhere. Determined to enjoy the rest of her stay, Abby pushed her unhappy thoughts of the future away.

As for having a sister packing up in her hotel room, that wasn't true, either. Grateful that he'd rescued her from an unwanted encounter, she'd instinctively gone into his arms. But she was still hesitant to confess she was alone.

Although a little voice whispered *caution*, she was beyond caring about the wisdom of spending the rest of the night with him. After all, what harm could there be in going for a walk? She was leaving tomorrow, and she'd never see him again.

Her thoughts quickly swung back to the horoscope she'd read on the plane coming to Mexico a week ago. The setting, the moonlight and the man beside her invited the kind of adventure that the horoscope had foretold. An adventure she was more than ready for.

Maybe it was because she didn't want to be alone to think about the birthday milestone that spelled a major turning point in her life. Or maybe it was because this man appeared to be totally unlike any man she'd ever known. Whatever the reason for her attraction to him, if there was ever a time and a place to let herself go, it was tonight—and here. Where no one knew her or cared what she did.

Taken with his low, full, sensuous voice, and lost in the invitation of his quirky smile, she nodded her agreement. "Thank you," she said. "I'd enjoy taking a walk with you."

"Thank *you*," he answered. He offered her his arm, and led her down the terrace steps to a curved walkway.

His fingers intertwined with hers; his hand was soft, warm and strong. Abby felt safe, secure and—strangely enough—cared for. For the first time since her divorce, years ago, she felt comfortable entrusting herself to a man she didn't know. She didn't stop to wonder why. If tonight was going to be a dream fulfilled, she intended to embrace every moment. Tomorrow could take care of itself.

They strolled down lamp-lit paths where sweet-smelling jasmine and vividly colored hibiscus bushes were in bloom. Under the glow of the flaming torches, his eyes seemed to twinkle with secret thoughts as they strolled along the cobblestone garden path. Drawn by his magnetic appeal, Abby stumbled.

"Here, let me help you."

She found herself surrendering to strong arms, brandy-colored eyes, and a voice laced with concern. She steadied herself with one hand on his broad shoulders. Looking up, she saw that he was younger than she was. And she noticed glints of gold in his brown hair. His quirky smile played on her heart strings, while his touch transformed the world around her to magic.

It was as if he became a figure out of a fairy tale. It didn't matter whether he denied being a knight in shining armor. Under the magic spell cast over them by the moonlight, he was surely a heroic figure. Even as she felt herself respond to his touch, Abby reminded herself that magic was an antidote to reality, and that she would surely awaken soon.

Still, her heart felt lighter than it had in months. Never one to give in to impulse, she felt tonight was her chance to be the young, carefree woman hidden inside her. For once in her life, she was going to throw reason to the wind. For tonight, more than ever before, she needed to believe in magic.

"Are you okay?" he asked. He tightened his hold around her waist and bent over to check her ankle. "Thank goodness, your ankle doesn't seem to be broken."

"I'm fine," she answered, a thousand miles from the truth. She was definitely not okay, not the way she was responding to the warmth of Logan Addams's arms and the genuine concern in his eyes. She sensed, gazing into his amber eyes, that he was no ordinary man. And that tonight was going to be a time to treasure.

"Hang on a minute," he said, steadying her with one hand. "Let me take off those shoes. You won't be needing them where we're going."

Abby shivered as his hands brushed her bare ankles and slipped off her high-heeled sandals. She gazed down at him while his warm hands wove their magic spell around her. If she followed him now, she sensed she'd be stepping into the fantasy world she had been longing for. Why else would she have flown off by herself to romantic Acapulco?

"Looking good," he finally said as he rose, his hand lingering on her heated skin. "Nothing wrong with you that I can tell."

Abby felt herself blush. Her senses awakened, she felt as if she couldn't get enough of the touch of his hands. Or of his reassuring smile. Whoever and whatever he was, she felt this was no ordinary meeting. Rather, it was one that fate had planned for her.

"Where are we going?" she asked when he tucked her shoes into his jacket pockets. It was a signal of ownership that sent pleasurable thoughts racing through her mind. Wherever they went, tonight, she wanted to belong to him.

JEFFREY ADDAMS LOGAN III gazed restlessly out of his office window as the wind-driven rain washed away the L.A. smog. Quite a change from the sun-drenched days and moonlit nights in Acapulco.

As Logan Addams—the name he used while traveling so no one could connect him with his well-known family name—he'd gone to the popular Mexican resort incognito. To take stock of himself, to come to grips with the reality of having to decide on his future. Instead, after three days he'd headed home with no ready answers. He hadn't intended to return so soon, but even Paradise would have lost its charm after that intriguing woman had left him sleeping on the tropical sands.

Scarlett.

He laughed softly as he whispered her name into the empty air. He knew her name was no more Scarlett than his was Logan Addams. He'd suspected she was putting him on, but he'd been so taken with her, he'd played her game.

From the moment he'd set eyes on this Scarlett, he'd been attracted to her fragile, golden beauty. He'd bided his time till he found an opportunity to finally meet her. And he'd remained with her when he'd found that she was not only beautiful, but intelligent and fun to be with. And not afraid to show her attraction to him.

Unlike so many women he knew, Scarlett had been a woman who didn't know or care who he was, or the net worth of his portfolio. She'd accepted

him at face value and made love with him with an
abandon that had matched his own. In the space of
a few hours, she'd made him laugh and groan with
pleasure while they'd escaped into a fantasy world.

What had started as an invitation to swim in warm
tropical waters had swiftly changed under his ex-
ploring hands and searching lips. The soft curve of
her hips seemed to have been made to fit against
him. Her waist had been only slightly larger than
the span of his hands, her flesh warm and vibrant.

What had followed had been a night of passion,
so tender and loving that it had swiftly become more
to him than a chance encounter.

Too bad he'd fallen asleep on the sand, and awakened to find her gone before he could be certain that
she'd been real and not just a dream.

He glanced at the well-known Logan Hotel logo
on the envelope which sat on the table where he'd
dropped it a week ago. He hadn't had to open it to
know its contents. After one look, he'd taken himself off to Acapulco—to think about his future, to
decide the road that future would take: pursuing his
own dreams of writing mysteries, or assuming the
management of the Logan hotel chain, which his
father insisted was his duty.

Now that Jeffrey had turned thirty, as he had re-
peatedly been reminded by his father, he was expected to make his choice. His father's choice, preferably. A choice he hadn't been able to voice.

Tonight, he was no closer to deciding than he'd been a week ago.

He sighed and turned away from the window. Maybe Scarlett had been running away from something, too. Maybe that was why she'd used an assumed name that no man in his right mind would have taken seriously. Whatever had brought her to Acapulco, he hoped when she'd returned home she at least would have been lucky enough to make her dreams come true.

He would have given up his heritage to know her real name and where she came from.

"ABBY CARSON! Well, thank goodness!" Nadine Williams jumped up from behind her desk and rushed to give Abby a careful once-over. After a big hug, she stepped back and surveyed Abby.

"Where have you been?" she scolded, now that she was apparently satisfied Abby was real and unharmed. "There we were, all of us, your family and friends all set to give you a fortieth birthday party, and you disappear without telling us where you were going! The note you left didn't say anything, only that you'd be back in a week! A week! Do you realize you've frightened us all half to death?"

Abby handed Nadine her raincoat and umbrella, wordlessly made her way into her own office, and closed the door firmly behind her. She wasn't ready to share her adventure. Not with Nadine and not with her family, either. Where she'd been and what she'd done was too precious to share.

As for a fortieth birthday, after overhearing whispered phone calls, a party had been exactly what she'd run from. Rather than face the celebration that would have reminded her of a milestone she'd rather ignore, she'd chosen to escape to the warmth and the beauty of Acapulco. There would be time enough to face reality later.

She'd flown off to Mexico to spend a quiet week alone, gathering her thoughts, making some plans of her own, now that her daughter was about to graduate college and go off on her own.

Instead, she'd found herself lost in the magical setting of the Concordia Hotel's garden fairyland and spending the night in a stranger's arms on the warm sands of Acapulco Bay—just as the horoscope had predicted. But she was no closer to coming to grips with making a new life for herself.

The adventure had left her with a memory that she could hold close, to warm her heart whenever reality set in. A memory so special, she couldn't voice it to anyone.

Shivering at the change in climate, Abby rubbed her arms to get warm. She went to a window and looked out at the latest El Niño storm that was spending its wrath over Los Angeles. The bleak picture of rain-slicked streets and stalled cars below, reminded her of the contrast between the gray skies of today and the brilliant sunshine she'd left behind in Acapulco. Of a night when moonlight and soft guitars had robbed her of her inhibitions and sent her into the arms of a man right out of a fairy tale—Logan Addams.

She turned back to her desk, shifted through the messages Nadine had given her, and shoved them away. All she could think of was the man she'd left sleeping on the beach in Mexico after a night that had exceeded her wildest dreams.

Logan had been different from the men she'd met in the years since her divorce, she thought wistfully. Young and virile, with a sense of self usually found in older men, he'd come to her rescue and invited her to walk into a fantasy world with him.

It hadn't taken long for her to realize there was an undeniable attraction between them, an unspoken understanding that somehow they'd been fated to meet. Strange, since he couldn't have been much more than thirty, and she had been so very aware of her own age that night.

The memory of exactly how she'd spent the night with him, first in warm waters and then on warm sands, sent heat through her middle.

"Abby, are you okay in there?" Nadine's voice sounded through the door.

"I'm fine," Abby answered, grateful that her secretary and friend was astute enough to keep her distance and to save her questions for later.

What had made her say yes to Logan in the first place? Abby wondered as she paced the office. Had it been the horoscope? Had it been the heat in Logan's eyes and their unspoken invitation that had been so tempting she couldn't resist? Or the realization that despite the age difference, he saw her as a desirable woman?

Critically, she gazed at her reflection in the window: five feet four inches; blond hair with a tinge of bronze; and five pounds too heavy in the hips. Certainly nothing remarkable, she thought as she turned sideways to get a better look at herself. So why had he chosen her out of all the available women at the world-famous resort?

She turned away from the window and gazed around the pristine businesslike office, so different from the tropical setting she'd found down south. The blue-and-gray setting, the cherry wood desk and chairs, and the Impressionist prints on the wall were pleasant and practical, but were nothing to dream over. She'd sold dreams in the form of homes to other people, but she hadn't managed to find a dream of her own—until Logan had appeared out of nowhere and had asked her to dance.

It was just as well she hadn't given Logan her real name or remained with him after she'd awakened. Somehow that made it easier to forget him, and he'd never be able to find her.

Abby sighed. It was time to put her romantic adventure behind her and face the reality of who she was and the job she had to do. Time to go back to concentrating on selling the luxurious real estate that had been her life for more than a dozen years. Time to forget Logan and their incredible night together.

It wasn't likely that would happen anytime soon. But at least, she thought suddenly, he'd been prepared that night so there was no way she could have become pregnant. That was the last thing she needed to worry about.

Chapter Two

Abby awakened with a groan and rubbed her stomach. Heavy late-night dinners were out, she thought ruefully—until she remembered she'd gone to bed without eating. She'd felt queasy and listless last night, just as she did now. Maybe it was a natural consequence of weeks of indulging in her sudden hunger for the highly spiced foods that she usually avoided. A hunger that began on that never-to-be-forgotten vacation in Mexico.

She was drifting back to sleep when she was jolted wide awake by a possibility that it was more than indigestion that was bothering her.

Could she be pregnant?

Twenty-one years had passed since her pregnancy with her daughter Kate, but the dizzy and nebulous feeling that had come with pregnancy was all too familiar.

Wide awake now, Abby curled on her side. Her eyes fastened on the combination digital clock/calendar that she kept on her nightstand to remind her of business appointments. A quick glance told her that it was six weeks to the day since she'd met a man named Logan Addams.

Abby swallowed and gazed thoughtfully at the calendar. When was her last period? She thought hard and realized it was about eight weeks ago. Could this strange feeling be the natural result of a single night of love? A night spent with a man whose magical charm had so captivated her that she'd ignored the small niggling voice in the back of her mind, warning that she might be headed for trouble?

Trouble? Trouble came in many guises, Abby thought as she examined the adventure she held close to her heart, but what had taken place between her and Logan hadn't been one of them.

But a baby at this stage in her life was something else!

Dismayed at the thought, Abby sank back against her pillows and contemplated her life. She had a successful career, a luxurious condominium and a shining new automobile fresh off the showroom floor. Her daughter, Kate, was about to graduate college and, finally, she would have time to indulge herself in her own interest in interior decorating. Perhaps even to consider marriage to her friend Sebastian Curtis—the man her own mother kept urging on her.

Abby gave up trying to go back to sleep, and spent the rest of the night mulling over her options if somehow it turned out she *was* pregnant.

For a woman like herself, the first option was out

of the question. Besides, she'd raised a daughter by herself before, and she could do it again.

But if her pregnancy was verified, did she have an obligation to try to find Logan and tell him she was expecting his child?

Abby knew how much Kate had missed having a full-time father. This baby deserved to be raised with a father too, preferably its own. But finding Logan was another matter.

The alarm clock finally rang. Time to stop daydreaming and begin to plan for tonight's annual gala dinner dance for the real estate community at the new Logan Wilshire Hotel.

"Mom? Are you awake?" Kate peeked around the door.

"Yes, sweetheart, come on in." Abby put aside her musings and patted the bed beside her. "I was just about to get up. Something wrong?"

"No, not really," Kate answered. "I was just wondering about the banquet tonight. Is Grandma coming with us?"

"Yes, of course." Abby smiled sympathetically. "You know you can't keep your grandmother away from a party. Not when she knows there are single men, music and dancing. She's so full of energy, sometimes I even feel as if I'm *her* mother."

"You aren't that old, Mom," Kate teased. "I've heard that forty is the prime of life. You still have plenty of time to meet the man of your dreams."

She'd already met the man of her dreams, Abby

thought with a smile, and, heaven help her, he may have left her with something to remember him by.

"It would be great to have a man around, instead of just the three of us showing up alone," Kate went on.

"I suppose so," Abby said as she lovingly brushed Kate's golden hair away from her face. "But if you're worried about not having anyone to dance with, I'm sure there'll be dozens of eligible men who will jump at the chance to dance with a pretty young girl like you."

"How about Sebastian? Do you think he would come along tonight if you asked him?"

"Sebastian?"

"Yes. You know, Sebastian Curtis." Kate eyed her mother as if Abby had come from another planet.

"Yes, of course." Abby stopped to consider the idea. Sebastian was a widower of her own age and a recent client. She'd found him an ideal condo high above the Wilshire corridor in Westwood several months ago, and during the process he'd become a friend. Maybe more than a friend, if what her mother had said about Sebastian's interest in Abby was true. "If you'd feel more comfortable having an escort, I suppose I could invite him to come along. I'll make a few calls."

"Gee, thanks, Mom." Kate bounced off the bed and made for Abby's closet. "How about lending me your new cocktail dress to wear tonight? You know, the black one that looks like a slip?"

Abby bit back a reply. The black dress Kate was referring to was the one Abby had worn on the enchanted night she'd met Logan. Because of the wonderful memories that surrounded the dress, she'd hung it at the side of her closet and hadn't worn it again. If she loaned it to Kate for tonight, what would Kate say if the dress still had sprinkles of sand in it?

Staring at her daughter, Abby suddenly realized that Kate had turned into a lovely young woman before her eyes. Definitely not a child anymore. Perhaps it *was* wise to ask Sebastian to escort them tonight—to keep Kate occupied.

"Of course," Abby finally answered. "Why don't you wear the pearls I gave you for your twenty-first birthday?"

"Great!" Kate slid open the closet doors, slipped the dress off the hanger, and held it to her while she modeled it in front of the floor-length mirror. A sultry smile passed over her face that made Abby blink.

"Thanks, Mom. Maybe now someone will realize I'm not a kid anymore!" She blew Abby a kiss as she disappeared through the bedroom door.

No, Abby agreed as she thought of the look that had come across her daughter's face. Kate was definitely not a child. She marveled at how quickly the years had passed since Kate's birth, and the thirteen years since she'd divorced Kate's father, Richard.

Oddly enough, she and Richard had become better friends than they'd been spouses. Easy to talk to, comforting to know, Richard periodically floated in

and out of their lives. It was at times like this that
Abby wished he were here to talk to. To exchange
thoughts about their daughter and the direction
Kate's life might be taking now that she was about
to finish her last year at college.

In fact, she and Richard were such good friends
that she wished he were here now to tell him about
the new wrinkle in her life—the baby she was in-
creasingly certain she was carrying.

She threw back the covers and got out of bed.
Maybe she ought to consider remarriage. To Richard, who had been showing a renewed interest in
her? To Sebastian, who had also shown an interest
in her and had almost become a member of her family? Perhaps tonight would be a good time to sound
Sebastian out. But she had one thing to take care of
first: a trip to the drugstore for an EPT kit.

FIVE MINUTES WERE UP.

Abby screwed up her courage and stared down at
the stick from the pregnancy test she held in her
shaking hand.

A plus sign. She *was* pregnant.

She had to admit the answer wasn't entirely unexpected, but it still came as a shock. Holding her
emotions at bay, she made a mental note to set up
a doctor's appointment to confirm the test results.

When she carried Kate, she'd waited for weeks
before her doctor agreed to take a "rabbit test" to
verify she was pregnant. Not so today. A few

minutes and a simple test, and the answer to her upset stomach was there.

She sat down on the edge of the bathtub and stared at the instrument of truth. Memories were coming to her so fast, she could hardly take it all in.

She recalled months of a queasy stomach, pain of childbirth, mounds of diapers, boiled bottles of formula, sleepless nights, cutting baby teeth, measles and day care. She recalled deciding to raise Kate on her own.

If motherhood hadn't been easy at age nineteen, what would it be like at forty?

THIS YEAR, the annual Realtor's Dinner Dance was sponsored by the Logan hotel chain and held at its new Wilshire Hotel on Wilshire Boulevard's miracle mile. The Logan Wilshire was part of the most successful and widely respected hotel chain in the country, if not the world.

"Lovely," Abby murmured, drawing Sebastian's attention to the lobby decorated in various shades of wine and gray, and the curving staircase that led up to the Grand Ballroom where the dinner dance was to take place. Shunning the crowded elevators, they made their way up the stairs to the second floor, where Italian imported marble pillars rose between walls of glass. In the background, the city lights twinkled against the backdrop of a black velvet night.

"Here, ladies, let me check your jackets," Sebastian offered. Abby smiled gratefully and handed him her long, cashmere cape.

"I think I'll keep mine on," Caroline Baker answered. "I don't want to catch a chill."

"Come on, Mother," Abby chided. "You know you'll be so busy dancing, you won't have time to catch anything. Except maybe a man."

Her mother smiled serenely. "You never know until you try, do you?" she said over her shoulder as she made her way to the ballroom.

"I wouldn't put it past Grandma," Kate giggled. "I'll bet as soon as she spots a man that interests her, she'll get him to ask her to dance."

"I know. She always manages to find someone, doesn't she?" Abby answered with a smile. "I'm sure tonight isn't going to be an exception."

"How about you, Kate?" Sebastian rested his hands on the shoulders of her velvet jacket. "May I?"

Abby noticed the way Kate blushed at his touch. How sweet, she thought idly as she gazed around for a familiar face. Kate might be twenty-one, but she was still young and vulnerable. It was a good thing she'd invited Sebastian to come along to keep an eye out for her.

"Do you know any of the Logan people?" Abby's mother inquired as they entered the ballroom.

"No, not yet," Abby answered as she checked the number of their table on the place card she'd been given at the door. "Their headquarters are in

San Francisco. I understand getting acquainted with the local realty board and its members is the primary purpose of their hosting the banquet this year. Why did you want to know?'' Abby spotted table number seventeen in the middle of the room. ''There's our table, over on the right.''

''I overheard someone say there'll be an announcement tonight concerning the young Logan heir.'' Caroline gazed around the room as she trailed behind Abby. ''I understand he's still young and single, and definitely just the man for Kate. If so, I'd like to meet him and arrange for Kate to meet him.''

Abby gestured to the chair beside hers. ''You just got here! When did you find the time to hear all that gossip?''

''Actually, Nadine told me,'' her mother said nonchalantly as she took her seat. ''She heard it from a friend of hers who has a friend who works here. She also says she's heard he's a real hunk.''

''Is there anything Nadine doesn't know?'' Abby laughed at her whimsical mother's choice of contemporary male descriptions. She glanced back, looking for Kate and Sebastian. They were trailing along, deep in conversation. Yes, Abby decided fondly, the courtly Sebastian obviously liked children. Not only would he be a good choice for a husband for her, he'd make a perfect second father for Kate. Of course, if the pregnancy test she planned on taking in the morning turned out to be accurate, she intended to be honest with him before she accepted his marriage proposal.

"Who's that good-looking young man over there?" her mother whispered.

Abby twisted in her seat to see the front of the dance floor where her mother was pointing. "Where?"

Abby's heart took a leap into her throat when the crowd parted. In a black, tailored tuxedo the man wore over his tanned and muscular body, he was easily one of the most handsome men she'd ever seen. The gesture he used to impatiently brush a lock of golden-brown hair away from his forehead was one she remembered. The crooked smile that hovered at the corner of his lips was familiar. It was the same smile that had seduced her.

It was Logan Addams.

Her pulse raced. Of all the places she might have expected to run into him, a local business association banquet wasn't it. Yet, under the glare of myriad overhead crystal chandeliers, it was clear that he was the same sexy man she'd met and left behind in Acapulco. And twice as appealing.

At one time she might have been happy to see him again, but not tonight. She was still trying to come to grips with the fact that she was pregnant with his child.

What would he say or do if he spotted her, she thought. Abby felt the immediate urge to flee, to get out of sight. The ladies' room was an option, but she couldn't possibly stay there for the rest of the night, could she? And she couldn't very well leave.

It would only bring unwanted questions from her mother and Kate.

"Abby?"

Her mother's voice and a tug on her arm brought Abby out of her bemused state. "Yes?"

"What's wrong with you? You're staring into space as if you've seen a ghost. If you keep that up, people will think something is the matter with you!"

Abby cringed inside. Being noticed was the last thing she wanted. She nervously undid her napkin from its fanciful fold, laid it across her lap, and averted her eyes from the front of the ballroom. Thankfully, the music started and diverted her mother's attention.

"I think I'll find someone to dance with," her mother announced as she started to push back her chair. Instead, her attention was riveted to the man who walked over to their table.

"Good evening, Miss Scarlett O'Malley. Great to see you again. May I have this dance?"

The voice was familiar—its tone, considering the man who owned it, all too intimate.

Logan!

Abby wanted to fade into the woodwork.

Her mother nudged her when Abby didn't reply. "Abby, dear, I think the gentleman is asking you to dance—although I don't understand why he's calling you by that ridiculous name," she went on to mutter into Abby's ear.

Abby raised her eyes to see the devil shining in Logan's smiling eyes. In the background, the melody that the orchestra began to play was the same one the violins and guitars had played the night she and Logan had danced in Acapulco. A song of a love lost and prayers it would be found again: "Lara's Theme." Abby's heart beat faster. The co-incidence of the song being played just as Logan was asking her to dance wasn't lost on her.

She hadn't forgotten the night Logan Addams had captured her imagination and made inroads into her heavy heart. From the warm expression in his soft eyes as he waited for her answer, she realized the night they'd spent together had meant something to him, too.

At her mother's prodding, Abby rose and took Logan's hand. She could feel everyone's curious eyes boring into her back, almost hear the question in her mother's. After this dance, she knew with an ache in the pit of her stomach, there would be an endless number of questions to answer.

"Well, Miss Scarlett O'Malley, you're the last person I expected to find here tonight," he said as he opened his arms and drew her onto the dance floor. "I've been thinking of you for weeks. I even thought of looking for you, but I didn't know where to start."

At the sound of his voice, Abby realized how empty the weeks had been since they'd been to-gether on the warm sands of Acapulco. Weeks when she'd felt alone and lonely, longing for the man who had taken her on a sensual voyage through a star-filled night.

She couldn't find the words to answer. She only knew it felt so right to be in his arms again, to have his arms around her, pressing her to his chest. To feel his warm breath against her skin as he whispered that ridiculous name she'd given him.

She kept her head hidden in his shoulder. How long would it be before he would find out who she really was? How long before he would confront her with her lie? Now that he was about to find out the truth, would he believe their time together had been the first time she'd ever done something so reckless, so uninhibited?

"No answer?" he asked into her hair as he swept her around the dance floor. "I was hoping you would tell me you've been thinking about me, too."

If only he knew. She had been thinking about him from the moment she'd walked away from him. And, since this very morning, about something that might send him running away from her.

"At any rate," he went on when she didn't answer, "now that I've found you, we'll have to become reacquainted. No more little white lies."

Now that he knew she hadn't told him the truth, a cold current ran through her at what he might think of her. Maybe he even thought she was used to one-night stands. At a loss for words, Abby managed some noncommittal remark.

"Was that was your family at your table?" he asked, interrupting her thoughts.

"Yes." That much, at least, was safe.

"Your husband?"

"No, a family friend."

"Not a fountain of information, are you?" he teased. "And the older woman," he added as he swung her around the floor in three-quarter time. "Your mother?"

"Yes." Abby shook herself. She'd never been a coward in her life and now was not the time to start. "Why?"

"When the dance is over, I hope you'll introduce me. I'm serious about wanting to know everything about you, you know. And I hope you'll want to get to know more about me."

Abby kept her silence. At the moment, she just wanted him to go away before her stomach rebelled.

"And the young girl seated at your table? You look so much alike, she must be your younger sister."

Abby swallowed hard. "Younger than you know," she answered. What would Logan think if he knew Kate was actually her daughter? To her relief, he nodded and held her more tightly than ever.

What was she going to do now? Abby wondered. Even if the achingly beautiful music hadn't done the trick, the strength of Logan's muscular body would have sent her senses rushing down the path they'd taken six weeks ago. A path that seemed to promise a fulfillment of dreams long denied.

"If I remember correctly, Scarlett O'Malley, your sister is wearing the same dress you wore the night we met." He was holding her so closely that she could feel the steady beat of his heart. When he smiled down into her eyes, she was lost.

"Tell her to take good care of the dress, because I'd like to see you in it again—and soon. The truth is, the dress has a special meaning for me," he said softly, "and I hope it does for you, too."

Abby smiled weakly. He'd left a reference to "together under tropical Mexico skies" unsaid, but the sensual message was there in his voice, his eyes. Before she had a chance to reply, a man wearing a Logan Hotel badge on his chest came up behind Logan, tapped him on the shoulder and murmured something in his ear.

Logan nodded, disappointment etched on his face.

"Sorry, Scarlett. I have to take an important telephone call. Here, let me walk you back to your table."

Visions of her mother taking over and asking Logan questions sprang to Abby's mind.

"Thank you, but you needn't bother. I'm sure you have other things to do."

"Oh, no, Scarlett O'Malley, not this time," he said with a grin. "I prefer to take you back to where I'll be able to find you again later. I shouldn't be long." He took her by the elbow and headed for her table.

The way Logan kept calling her Scarlett O'Malley was enough to make Abby wish they hadn't met tonight, after all. The last thing she wanted to have to do was introduce him to her mother. Like Nadine, Caroline Baker was too curious for her own good and just as adept at spreading gossip, or asking blunt questions for which Abby had no ready answers.

"I really need to visit the ladies' room to freshen up. I'm sure I'll see you around later," Abby said politely. At his reluctant nod, she moved in the direction of the rest room with all the dignity she could muster.

"WHO WAS THAT MAN and where did he go?" Caroline asked when Abby came back to the table. "He's so handsome and so very sexy. Personable, too," she said thoughtfully. "I can't imagine why he wasn't wearing a wedding ring. You don't see many of his kind on the loose."

"I thought you wanted to dance," Abby muttered, glancing around the table for bread or crackers, anything to settle her roiling stomach. If this kept up, even soda crackers weren't going to keep her from embarrassing herself.

"Later," her mother answered. "Right now, I'm dying to know who that young man is."

"No one special," Abby answered. "Just someone I met on my vacation." She started to reach for a badly needed glass of wine, but dropped her hand when she remembered alcohol was a no-no for an expectant mother. After her dance with Logan, the multitude of curious eyes on her weren't helping settle her stomach—or her nerves.

"And you've kept quiet all this time about meeting such a great-looking young man? Abby, how could you? Now," her mother said as she leaned closer, "tell me everything you know about him."

"Not very much," Abby answered, taking a sip of ice water to calm her nerves. *Only that he was brave and kind and persuasive. Very. That his body was strong and masculine and, under the light of a tropical moon, the color of copper. And that his brandy-colored eyes and deep velvety voice were able to perform feats of magic that made an ordinary woman feel like a fairy princess.*

"At least tell us how you met him," her mother insisted. "And why he called you by that ridiculous name, Scarlett O'Malley?"

Abby couldn't tell her mother that Logan had stepped in and saved her from unwelcome advances from a stranger. Or that she'd been the victim of an overactive imagination—after all, the stranger had only asked her to dance. Logan had been a stranger, too.

She warmed as she remembered how quickly he'd become a great deal more than a friendly stranger.

How could she possibly confess she'd used an impossible name like Scarlett O'Malley to avoid anyone finding or remembering her? Big mistake. Everyone was going to remember the name, her mother included. She should have chosen a more prosaic name, like Mary Smith.

She gazed around the table from Kate's avid eyes to Sebastian's mild look of surprise. Good Lord, she thought. What would they think of her if they knew the truth?

Abby was sure she was never going to be able to get through this night.

"It was just a joke, Caroline," she managed, breaking a dinner roll into pieces to keep her fingers from trembling. Her stomach started to rebel again. Why hadn't she thought to bring along dry soda crackers in her evening bag? If she had a stomach upset now, her possible pregnancy was going to become the greatest joke of all. And just as unexplainable as Logan Addams's interest in her.

Mentally, she kept her fingers crossed during dinner, hoping that Logan was involved in some kind of business that would keep him from coming back to find her as he'd promised.

An old friend of her mother's, Arnold Bates, claimed her mother for a dance just in time. Abby breathed a sigh of relief when Caroline floated away in a cloud of peach-colored chiffon. Abby accepted automatically when Sebastian, with his old world courtesy, bowed and asked her to dance. She glanced at Kate, who smilingly waved her away.

The dance was a familiar two-step, sung by a well-known ballad singer and backed by a trio of blending voices. The amplification system kept Sebastian silent after a few courteous exchanges about the music and the luxurious setting, thank goodness. All she could think about was Logan Addams. To her surprise, she was actually relieved when the dance was over and Sebastian escorted her back to their table.

She glanced at him now, engrossed in listening to

Kate's chatter with a fond smile. Why was she so suddenly reluctant to have him ask her to marry him? Abby wondered. A short time ago, even as far back as when she'd escaped to Acapulco, she had been considering accepting his marriage proposal. Now, she was suddenly doubtful that the sweet and charming Sebastian Curtis was the man she wanted to marry.

All she could think of was Logan's smile, and the way he'd appeared out of nowhere to turn her predictable life upside down.

Her mother's voice shook her out of her reverie.

"Abby Carson, why couldn't you have told me— your own mother—the truth?"

Abby pulled herself together and searched her memory for any white lies she might have told her mother. Outside of hiding her romantic interlude in Mexico, her conscience was clear. "The truth about what?"

"About Jeffrey Addams Logan III, that's what," her mother exclaimed as she dropped into her seat. She gazed reproachfully at Abby. "Imagine, pretending not to recognize him, when most women would give their eyeteeth just to know a man like that!"

"I don't *know* anyone called Jeffrey Addams Logan III," Abby insisted. She gazed around the huge ballroom at the dozens of guests milling around— some familiar, some not. "I've never met him."

Her mother's incredulous expression would have been laughable under any other circumstances, but somehow Abby sensed it wasn't the time for laughter. Not when the similarity between the name Logan had given her and the one by which her mother was calling him began to ring a bell.

Chapter Three

Abby struggled to keep her equilibrium as the room started to spin around her. If her mother was right, Logan's true identity would explain some of the things she'd noticed during the evening.

The way he had obviously been able to get the orchestra leader to play "their song." And to time it so perfectly.

And the deference shown him by the man who'd called him away for an important telephone call.

And Logan's air of confidence—definitely not that of a mere guest.

But the owner of the Logan hotel chain? No way!

"You have to be mistaken, Caroline. The man I danced with is Logan Addams. He's the man I met in Mexico."

"I am not mistaken," Caroline insisted. "Arnold Bates just told me who your friend is. He's known Jeffrey Addams Jr. for years, and has met the man's son a number of times! Imagine my chagrin when Arnold was curious about how well you knew Jeffrey."

Jeffrey *Addams* Logan! Logan Addams? Of course. How could she not have guessed the truth as soon as her mother had mentioned his name?

How could she have been so taken in by his seductive manner and sweet talk in Acapulco, let alone tonight?

How could she have made such a fool of herself?

Her head pounding, Abby suddenly felt as if she were being drawn into a whirlpool, pulling her deeper and deeper into its darkness.

"Mother!"

Faintly, Abby could hear Kate's voice calling to her. Someone pressed a cold, dampened napkin against Abby's forehead. She struggled to pull herself together. "I'm okay, Kate," she whispered. "Please, don't make a scene."

Abby's mother's voice sounded briskly in the background as she massaged Abby's shoulders. "Now, Abby, take a deep breath and keep your head down. You'll be fine in a moment."

Abby groaned. If the state of affairs was as she suspected, she wasn't going to be fine for seven more months.

Why had he chosen to deliberately hide his true identity? Why had he drawn her into a relationship that had no chance of going anywhere—even if she had remained in Acapulco a few more days as he'd asked her to?

The man was born to wealth and power. She was a nineties' career woman who worked to support herself, her daughter and her mother. She was a woman without a prestigious family background or the wealth to match his. And, most important of all, as far as she could tell, she was a woman at least ten years older than he was.

By the time Abby's head had cleared, she was honest enough to admit she had no right to call the kettle black. It didn't matter why Logan had hidden his true identity in Acapulco—it had been his business. She hadn't been honest with whatever-his-name-was, either. She'd hidden her own identity as well.

"Pardon me, ladies, Sebastian, I have someone here who would like to be formally introduced to all of you."

Abby looked up from her clenched hands to see her mother's friend, Arnold Bates, gazing down at her. His eyes sparkled as if he were enjoying a private joke. At his side, with a definite twinkle in his own eyes, stood the man she'd known intimately as Logan Addams.

The situation might be amusing to them, she thought sourly, but as far as she was concerned, what was happening to her tonight was a nightmare.

She reached for her glass of water, just in case.

"Caroline, I'd like to introduce you to Jeffrey Logan. Jeff, I'd like you to meet my good friend Caroline Baker, her daughter Abby Carson and her granddaughter Kate Carson."

Abby took a deep swallow of ice-cold water.

Her mother glowed as she acknowledged the introduction. "And this is our dear friend, Sebastian Curtis," she added graciously.

"I'm pleased to meet all of you," Logan-Jeffrey said with a broad smile, "but please, call me Jeff." His smile and a quirked eyebrow were directed squarely at Abby. "When I mentioned I was looking for a home to lease or purchase, Ms. Carson, Arnold here told me you were definitely the person to see."

Even though her stomach was churning and the voices around her were growing faint again, Abby managed to hide her dismay. Her heart took a dive. She drew a deep breath and managed to say, "Some other time, if you don't mind."

"No problem," he answered agreeably. "Arnold gave me your business card. I can stop by your office tomorrow morning."

Tomorrow morning?

Slowly but surely, and under everyone's scrutiny, Abby felt her ordered life unravel. From the corner of her eye, Abby could see her mother, Kate and Sebastian waiting for her reaction. She took another sip of cold water to clear her head.

"In the meantime, Ms. Carson," Jeff said, moving to her side and holding out his hand, "shall we finish our dance?"

Abby was about to refuse when she felt the full force of her mother's elbow against her ribs. "Of course," she answered, rising to her feet. Dancing with the heir to the Logan fortune was preferable to being black and blue all over.

"So, I turned out to be right, after all. Scarlett

O'Malley isn't your real name,'' Jeff murmured in her ear as he glided with her around the dance floor. "Frankly, I suspected as much from the beginning, but I wanted to see how far you would go with the masquerade. Do you mind telling me—why the assumed name?"

Abby fought for time and for her rebellious stomach to settle. To her dismay, it was beginning to look as if she became nauseated every time she was under stress. "Only if you tell me why you chose to use a false name."

"Simple," he answered frankly. "I was there hoping for some private time and trying to make a decision that could affect the rest of my life. I didn't want anyone to know where I was or who I was. If my actual identity got out, my father would have been on the telephone in minutes. But," he added as he looked down into her eyes, "I would have told you the truth in the morning if you hadn't disappeared."

"Why me?" Drawn by the depth of feeling in his eyes, Abby's initial dismay began to fade.

"I had the feeling you were meant to become an important part of my life." He gazed down at her with a rueful smile. "I thought I explained that to you the night we met. From the way you left before I awakened, I take it you didn't believe me?"

"No, how could I? It sounded like a typical line men come up with when they want to impress a woman," Abby answered frankly. "Besides, how could I take you seriously? We didn't even know each other.'' As soon as her words left her lips, she blushed. They may have been strangers when they met, but before the night was over they'd known each other in the biblical sense. She bravely returned the knowing look in his eyes.

What in heaven's name did he think of her now?

"But you liked me in spite of my 'line,' didn't you?" he teased. "Otherwise…" He left the rest of the sentence unsaid. But Abby knew exactly what he meant.

Liking him had been the least of her reactions to him that night. Embarrassed, Abby tried to change the subject. "You said you went to Acapulco looking for answers. Did you manage to find what you were looking for?"

"Depends on which questions you were referring to," he answered, swinging her away from another dancer's intrusive elbow. "Before the day was over, I'd added a few new ones. Too bad you weren't there to answer them."

"You said some of the answers would decide your future," she pressed, ignoring his innuendo. "Isn't that what you said brought you to Acapulco?"

"True enough. And no, I wasn't able to resolve anything. And awakening to find you gone only added one more dilemma for me to resolve," he answered in a voice full of not-so-hidden meanings.

Abby felt herself color, a childish habit she hadn't been able to outgrow. "I really didn't have a choice," she murmured. "Even the best of fairy tale vacations has to end."

"Fair is fair," Jeff replied. "I've told you the truth about myself and why I used an assumed name. Now, it's your turn." He gazed at down at her reflectively. "By the way, since I take it there was no sister waiting for you, what were you doing alone in Acapulco?"

Abby tried to smile. "Truthfully, I guess I was running away, too."

"From whom or from what?" Jeff asked, motioning for the orchestra leader to continue playing. "It looks to me as if you have a lot going for you: family, friends, and, from what I hear, a successful career. Not a bad guy in sight."

How could Abby tell him that she'd run away from having to face her fortieth birthday—a weighty milestone for a woman. Or the decision to accept Sebastian's marriage proposal and to settle down to a safe, predictable life?

Still, now that he'd just been so open with her, it was a time for honesty. "Growing older, I guess."

"Older?" His gaze swept her. "Surely not the way you looked that night. Or tonight, for that matter. What brought that on?"

"The night we met was my birthday."

"I wish you'd told me," Jeffrey said. "I would have helped you celebrate."

"You did," she said, dimpling in spite of herself. "More than you know."

If he only knew, he'd helped celebrate her birthday in a manner most women only dream of.

And in the process he might even have left her with a birthday present that would remind her of him every day of her life....

"Besides, I'm past the age of wanting to celebrate birthdays," she added with a light laugh.

"Nonsense," he answered. He swept her with an admiring glance, then smiled reassuringly. "I have eyes to see, and I can add, Scarlett O'Malley. Let me be the first to tell you, you're not old. Based on the little I do know about you, I think you're younger in here than you think you are." His fingers fleetingly brushed a spot over her heart before he reclaimed her hand and swung her into another slow set of music.

"Don't you think you ought to start calling me Abby? Everyone will think you're out of your mind if you keep calling me Scarlett."

"Nope. If you don't mind, I'd like to call you by that name—at least when we're alone. It reminds me of the blithe spirit I met in Acapulco. If it comes to that, you can tell anyone who asks that it's a private joke."

It might have been a private joke, Abby mused, but if he kept this up, it wasn't going to be private for long. Still, she was pleased. She'd never thought of herself as a blithe spirit, except for that one wonderful night when she'd had enough of being Abby Carson. Although, like the fictional Scarlett, there might be a price to pay.

She leaned into his solid chest, lost herself in the masculine feel of him, the firm pressure of his leading hand on her back, and the sound of his deep voice humming to the music. Maybe he was right about her being younger than she thought, at least in spirit. Why else would she have dared to take up the challenge in her horoscope that had sent her into his arms?

Between laughter and loving, it had been a night when the prim and proper Abby Carson had accepted a prophecy in a newspaper horoscope and emerged a changed woman.

"So, Scarlett, where do we go from here?"

Abby wasn't sure.

She gazed up into the winning smile, and the invitation in his eyes warmed her.

"I don't really know," she answered truthfully.

"Why not pick up where we left off? I thought we could have some fun together."

"Maybe because this isn't a tropical paradise."

The lips that brushed her forehead in answer threatened to rob her of any further pragmatic explanation, but she had to try. "The moon here in Los Angeles doesn't give off the same magic as it does in Mexico. Somehow, life here seems more real."

"Reality is what we make it," Jeff said, abruptly leading her off the dance floor and into the privacy of a small service area. His hand that held hers was firm and strong, his step decisive. "It doesn't matter if we're on a warm tropical island or here in Los

Angeles. The reality is that I want to see you again, to get to know you. And," he added, smiling into her eyes, "if you feel the same way about me, nothing else matters."

"Except for one important thing," Abby answered. "A few minutes ago, you said you can count. Surely you must realize I'm older than you are."

"What does age matter if we care about each other?" He glanced over her head. "Turn around and take a look at your daughter, and notice the way she's looking at Sebastian Curtis."

Abby turned and took a long look at Kate and Sebastian, their heads together deep in conversation, the party around them forgotten. Lately, she'd been under the impression Sebastian was interested in *her!* She'd even gone so far as to look at him as a suitor whose proposal she was on the verge of accepting.

As for Kate, Abby recalled her saying early that morning that if she wore Abby's black slip dress, there was someone who wouldn't think she wasn't old enough. Old enough for what? And was Sebastian that "someone" she'd wanted to impress with her grown-up state?

Abby shook her head. "To tell the truth, I've never seen him look at Kate that way."

"Maybe it's because you haven't looked closely at the two of them lately."

"You have to be mistaken," Abby protested. "Sebastian is my age."

"That's the point I was trying to make," Jeff replied, cupping her cheek with his hand. "When two people care about each other, age doesn't make a difference."

Abby wished that she could believe he was right. It might not matter to him now, but he was bound to think about it more realistically sooner or later. Better sooner.

"Nonsense," Abby said firmly. "Sebastian is merely a good friend to Kate."

"Sure." Jeff laughed softly. "If that's your idea of 'friendship,' I'm more than willing to be that kind of a friend of yours. At least until I have a chance to convince you that age doesn't matter. But I'm warning you, you had me under your spell the moment I laid eyes on you. And if you let yourself get to know me, maybe you'll get to feeling the same way about me."

He caressed her chin, ran his fingers over her lips. "Want to seal our friendship with a kiss?"

"Be serious and take me back to my table," Abby said, glancing nervously around her. Everyone's eyes seemed to be on her. She took a deep breath when her rebellious stomach threatened to protest. "I think it's time for me to go home."

"It's still early. There's dinner and a few formalities still ahead." His expression changed when he took a second look at her. "What's the matter? Aren't you feeling well?"

"I'm fine." Abby added another white lie to a list growing longer by the hour. But she *did* have to get out of here before stress turned her stomach inside out.

She glanced at her watch. "I can't wait for dinner or any formal ceremonies. I have to be at work early tomorrow morning."

He made no attempt to hide his disappointment. "Tomorrow is Saturday. I thought we might spend the day together—do something special and get reacquainted."

Abby felt herself grow warm at the thought of what "something" he had in mind.

"I'm sorry, I can't." She broke free of his hold. "In the real estate business weekends are the busiest days of all."

WHEN ABBY ARRIVED at her office the next morning, she saw Jeff waiting for her in Nadine's office. She took a deep breath and paused in the doorway to collect her thoughts. Nadine, bless her curious heart, had poured him a cup of her special blend of coffee and was offering him a plate of poppy seed cookies—a specialty she reserved for a few select clients. And a sure sign that she intended to find out everything she could about Jeff.

Poor Jeff. If he could take Nadine's strong, black coffee, he didn't stand a chance of getting away without Nadine's third degree.

"So tell me, Mr. Logan," Nadine purred, "what brings you to Los Angeles, and how long do you intend to stay?"

"I'm actually a native, Miss Williams, but I travel

a great deal.'' He paused to bite into a cookie. "Delicious! As to how long I intend to remain here this time, that depends.''

"Please, call me Nadine. I have a feeling we're going to see a lot of each other. Can I freshen up your coffee?'' At his bemused nod, she reached for the coffeepot. "Exactly what does your stay depend on?''

"It depends on—''

Abby had heard enough. "Thank you, Nadine. I'll take over now,'' Abby said briskly. She hung her coat on the tree rack and led the way into her office. If she left Nadine to her inquisition, heaven only knew what kind of intimate questions she would be asking next.

"Why don't you bring your coffee into the office, Mr. Logan,'' she said, formal under Nadine's curious eyes, "and tell me what kind of accommodations you're looking for.''

Jeff winked at Nadine and smothered a grin behind another bite of his cookie. Abby might want to keep their relationship a secret, but as for himself, he had nothing to hide. He was attracted to Abby, pure and simple.

"I'm tired of staying at hotels,'' he answered as he followed Abby into her office. "I am thinking about leasing a furnished house with an option to buy. It all depends on how things work out.''

Abby nodded, took a seat behind her desk and opened her portfolio. "How large a place were you looking for?''

"Again, that depends on how things work out," he repeated pointedly.

Abby's stomach fluttered.

"Did you have a particular neighborhood in mind?"

"Not particularly. Any suggestions?"

Abby frowned and looked across the desk at him. "You're not being much of a help, Mr. Logan. If you can't tell me what type of place you're looking for, I'm not sure I can help you."

Jeff smiled pleasantly. "Please call me Jeff. As for a place to call home, for now, primarily, I need a place to work when I'm not at the Logan Wilshire."

Abby had visions of him as a painter in his free time away from the hotel business. If so, he needed a house with a studio with lots of light. "How much space will you need for your...painting, is it—?"

"Not much. Actually, I'm a writer. I write mystery novels."

"How interesting," she answered politely, revising the size of a home downward. All he needed was space for a computer. Still, obviously money wasn't the object. "Have you been published?"

"Not yet," he said with a hopeful grin, "but I'm thinking of giving it more of my attention. Like all about-to-be-published writers, I have high hopes I'll get a break soon."

Abby nodded. "Rumor has it that you are going to take over part of the management of the Logan hotel chain. I understood you were going to make an announcement at the Realtor's dinner. Was the announcement made after I left?''

"Rumors, Scarlett, purely rumors. Don't believe everything you hear." He set the empty coffee cup on a side table, leaned back in his chair and studied her. "You might say, I'm the black sheep in my family. Or, the way I see it, the most independent one. My father intends to retire soon and wants me to follow in his footsteps by taking over the active management of the new Logan Wilshire. Actually, having to make that decision was what sent me to Acapulco."

"And you still haven't made up your mind about entering the hotel business?"

"No, not yet."

Abby wondered if it was his dream of becoming a published writer that kept him from joining his father. She understood having a dream and wanting to pursue it. She'd done that herself—but out of necessity. At least, until impulse had taken her to Acapulco. Of course, Jeff obviously had the luxury of choice.

Jeff Logan reminded her of her ex-husband, Richard, an actor experiencing ups and downs at the time of their divorce. More downs than ups, she recalled. Granted, Richard was now a successful theater critic, but it had taken him years to find a niche. Poor and impractical though he might have been, Richard at least had known what he wanted. Jeff, wealthy though he might be, still couldn't make up his mind about his future.

Now that she had secured her own future, she'd had more than enough experience with life's uncertainties without adding to them.

She leafed through her listings. "I have a furnished property in Westwood that might do. There's a minimum year's lease with an option to buy. You can pick up the option at any time."

"Fine, go ahead and draw up a lease. If you like the property, I'm sure I will, too."

"I prefer you look at it before you make up your mind," Abby answered firmly. She glanced at her watch. "I have an hour or so before my next client arrives. Shall we?"

THE WHITE CAPE COD wooden home, with the green shutters that had been so popular in Westwood thirty years ago, was sheltered from its neighbors by a white picket fence. A riot of colorful spring flower beds bordered the brick walk to the house. A graceful weeping willow brooded over the front lawn.

Inside the living room, bright yellow-and-blue fabric covered a large couch and two matching love seats. Nutmeg-colored pine occasional tables and a coffee table competed for space. Huge bookcases covered one wall. The room was lit by shafts of golden sunlight shining through a dozen paned windows and the French door leading to an outdoor patio.

"Nice," Jeff announced when they returned to the living room after a tour of the three bedrooms, a large den and a state-of-the-art kitchen. "It doesn't look as if anyone has ever lived here, does it?"

"The house has been here for years, but the current owners only recently redecorated. The husband was transferred overseas for an indefinite stay, so they decided not to take the furniture with them."

"Lucky me," Jeff said, opening the refrigerator. "Say, they've left a bottle of wine. Shall we celebrate?"

"No, thanks," Abby answered. "Not at this time of the morning." She couldn't tell him that wine was a no-no for a possibly pregnant woman. "We can fill out the forms back at the office. Actually, I was sure you'd like the house," Abby added. "Look over there. This ought to inspire you." She led him to the French doors, which in turn led to a covered patio and a beautifully landscaped backyard. In the center, there was a large shimmering swimming pool.

Jeff came up behind and brushed her cheek with the back of his hand. "I have all the inspiration I need—right here."

He was becoming too close for comfort, Abby thought as she tried to draw away. "I thought you wrote mysteries."

"I do." He turned her around, lifted her chin and ran his finger over her lips. "Romantic mysteries. And, at the moment, I'm tempted to do some research."

A flush swept through Abby as her eyes locked with his. Her toes, and a few more intimate places, warmed to his frank admiration. For a brief moment, she was swept with the temptation to lose herself in his arms and to recapture the hours they'd spent in Acapulco. Until she realized that if she gave in to that temptation, she might be getting herself into more than they both were prepared to handle.

The practical side of her warred with her hidden passionate side. Her senses warned her he might be another man like her former husband—a dreamer without a connection to reality. A man she couldn't afford to have at this stage in her life.

Abby told herself this was merely another business visit. No matter how she responded to Jeff, a signed lease was all that she was here for.

"Abby, what's wrong?" Jeff asked, as she drew away and turned back into the bedroom where she'd left her portfolio. He followed her.

"Nothing, and everything," she answered, avoiding looking at the king-size bed. "In spite of what you may think of me, I don't make it a habit of falling into bed with the first man I'm attracted to."

"Ah, so you admit you're attracted!" Before she could answer, he grabbed her and hugged her so hard she was afraid her ribs might break. "That makes two of us. I'm attracted to you, too."

"For all the wrong reasons, I'm afraid."

"What could be wrong about this?" He gently lifted her face up to his and kissed her. "And this," he said as he kissed her again. "I can't get you out of my mind, Scarlett O'Malley, and I'm not ready to try."

Abby's heartbeat gathered speed with each kiss, each time he pressed her closer to him. He tasted of coffee and cookies, and throbbed with masculine desire. A desire that matched her own. She had to will herself to remember there were still many questions to ask, questions to answer. The issues between them that loomed larger than life—the difference in their ages, and his still undecided plans for his future.

She wasn't even sure where she would fit into that future, if at all.

"Jeff, please." Abby pulled out of his embrace. "I'm not sure what you want of me. For that matter, I'm not even sure what I have to give you. We're people from two different worlds who see life differently."

"It's simple, really. In spite of this—" he touched her tender lips "—for now, I just want to get to know you," he answered. "To have you get to know me. To find out if what we feel for each other is real. That's not asking too much, is it?"

"Jeff…" she warned.

"Truce," he said. His eyes softened and he took her back into his arms. "Let's make a truce," he whispered against her lips. "For now, let's be friends."

Abby's good intentions vanished.

Chapter Four

Back in her office again, Abby found her secretary waving a sheaf of messages. "Looks as if your social life is about to pick up," Nadine gloated. "Half of the calls were from people who want to invite you to parties. And—" she grinned as she handed the yellow slips of papers to Abby "—they want you to bring Jeffrey Logan with you. Sounds to me as if you two have become the hottest twosome in town."

Abby silently took the messages. After spending the morning fighting off his magnetism, the last thing Abby wanted to do was discuss Jeff with Nadine or anyone else. What she *did* want to do was closet herself in her office and think about the future.

Jeff had asked to be friends, Abby thought wryly. It wasn't going to be easy to remain merely friends after the night in Mexico and the way they obviously still felt about each other. But she had agreed to try.

"And the other half of the telephone calls?" Abby hung up her coat, thought about a cup of strong, black coffee, then changed her mind. Just the smell of coffee seemed to upset her stomach lately. She reached for a packet of soothing lemon herbal tea and hoped for the best.

"From your mother. She wants to know how the morning went with Mr. Logan."

Abby added hot water to her cup, let the tea bag brew, and stared at Nadine. "How did she know he was here?"

"Caroline manages to know everything that's going on," Nadine answered with a nonchalant shrug.

"Could she have heard it through a grapevine?"

"She only asked me where you were and when you were coming back," Nadine said defensively. "It sounded as if she wanted to talk to you about something important. Besides, you wouldn't want me to lie to your mother, would you?"

"It all depends on the subject," Abby replied. "When it comes to Jeff Logan, the answer is 'yes.'" She started into her office. "But if it makes you feel better, consider it a white lie."

"Oh, one more thing, Abby. There was a return telephone call from Dr. Gardner's office. There's been a cancellation. You can have a two-fifteen appointment tomorrow, if you're interested. Want me to call back and confirm it for you?"

At the reminder that the inevitable moment of reckoning was at hand, butterflies in Abby's stomach took flight. The EPT she'd taken yesterday morning had been a true reading. Fighting off the feeling of nausea, she sipped the hot tea to calm her nerves and thought of the old Mexican saying, *Que será, será*—Whatever will be, will be. While she was certain Jeff had used protection in Mexico, it was too late to start worrying about it now. "No thanks, I'll take care of it myself."

"Abby, are you okay? You haven't been your old self since you got back from your vacation."

Abby looked back over her shoulder. There was genuine concern in her secretary's voice. Nadine might be a pain in the neck on occasion, but she meant well. "I'm fine, thanks. It's only that I didn't sleep too well last night."

Abby sighed as she went into her office and closed the door behind her—a signal that she didn't want to be disturbed. She paused to look at herself in a decorative wall mirror. Nadine's question was one she would undoubtedly have to answer again and again in the next seven months. That, and the inevitable "Who's the father?"

"CONGRATULATIONS, ABBY. If your tests turn out as I'm sure they will considering how healthy you are, I'd say you're about six or seven weeks along into a healthy pregnancy. We'll have you take an amniocentesis soon just to make sure everything is okay."

Numb, Abby stared at her gynecologist and long-time friend, Beth Gardner. The pregnancy wasn't a surprise, but hearing it confirmed still came as a shock to her system.

"Thank you, I think," Abby mumbled as she struggled into her clothing and buckled the belt to her skirt. It might have been her imagination, but the skirt felt a little tighter than before.

"It's been twenty-one years since your last pregnancy, Abby," Beth went on briskly, checking Abby's chart. "Things have changed since then. It might be a good idea if you brought the lucky father along with you on your next visit. I'd like to explain what the two of you can expect in the coming months."

"No, thanks," Abby murmured, knowing full well what the next seven months would bring. Her eyes glazed over at the thought. "I'm in this one by myself."

"Yourself?" Beth chided playfully. "Come on now, Abby, we both know it takes two to make a baby."

"To be honest with you, Beth, the man doesn't know he's going to be a father."

"And you don't want to tell him?"

"Not yet." *And maybe never.*

Beth shrugged. "It's your call, Abby. But, if nothing else, sooner or later you'll have to decide whose name you're going to put on the birth certificate. As I said before, things have changed since you had Kate. Here's a list of dos and don'ts. Call me right away if you experience any of the adverse symptoms on the list. Now," she added briskly, "I usually like to see my older patients every three weeks. Have my office nurse give you an appointment. Oh, and by the way, don't forget to get in some light exercise."

Older patients! Considering how she was already worried over the age difference between herself and Jeff, the reminder was the last thing Abby needed! She glanced at the two-page list. Most of the food she liked to eat was on the no-no list. The spicy Mexican dishes she craved, although okay in moderation, upset her stomach. The recommended "good stuff" on the list was largely grains, fruits and green leafy vegetables. The rest sounded less appealing than baby food. She folded the list, stuffed it in her purse and rose to leave.

Beth followed her to the door. "Good luck, Abby. If I were you, I'd give your man a break and tell him the good news. I don't care how liberated you are, there's no reason to go through this pregnancy by yourself. Besides, the man might want to know he's going to be a father."

"ARE YOU SURE everything's okay?" Nadine asked cautiously, when Abby wandered back into the office. After a close look at Abby's pale face, she shook her head. "You look worse than you did before. Did the doctor find something wrong with you?"

Abby glanced glumly at Nadine. "No, I'm fine. *But the rabbit died*," she added under her breath.

"What did you say?"

"Nothing important," Abby said briskly. "Did you call and change my appointments for this afternoon?"

"Yep. Told them you'd call and reschedule as

soon as you got back. And, oh, yes, your mother is still looking for you. Sebastian, too."

"Sebastian?"

"Yes. He said he could drop over to see you anytime. Just call him whenever you have time."

A visit from Sebastian was the last thing she needed to face right now, Abby thought as she closed the door behind her and reached for her appointment book. On the other hand—she dialed the first telephone number on the while-you-were-out slip only to hear a voice on an answering machine— maybe Sebastian *was* what she needed.

When he'd dropped her off the other night, he'd hinted that he wanted to talk to her about something important. In fact, now that she took the time to think about it, he'd hinted that he wanted to speak to her several times over the past few days. She'd put him off because she hadn't been ready for his marriage proposal.

Sebastian was a genuinely nice man, she thought wistfully. And she was fond of him. She was. Just not fond enough to spend the rest of her life growing old with him. Not when an inner voice whispered that after meeting Jeff, she wasn't ready to grow old.

Her mother and Kate seemed to like Sebastian, too. Especially Kate. And from the way he'd fussed over Kate lately, he was obviously the fatherly type.

But not the romantic and exciting man her horoscope had predicted would find her. He was not Jeff Logan.

Maybe the time *had* come to hear Sebastian and to put Jeff and the interlude in Mexico behind her.

But not today.

First, she needed time to get used to the idea of becoming a mother at this stage of her life.

Abby glanced at the souvenir paperweight on her desk she'd brought back from Mexico; a red hibiscus flower preserved in a square plastic cube. She'd bought the souvenir because the flower reminded her of moonlit hotel gardens and a night spent in the arms of a secret lover.

She picked up the cube and ran a gentle finger over it. Slow-motion scenes of herself and Jeff, with limbs entwined under a moonlit sky on warm sands, floated across her mind's eye. She could almost feel the warm, gentle breeze that had blown over them as he'd held her in his arms and made passionate love to her. Hear the soft sound of the ocean as it rippled to shore in Acapulco Bay, and the faint echoes of guitars and violins floating through a velvet night.

It seemed strange that Jeff hadn't noticed the souvenir flower or commented on its presence on her desk when he'd been in her office that morning. It was true that women were more sentimental than most men, but surely the magical night they'd spent together must have meant something to him as it did her. But, maybe not.

All the more reason to consider Sebastian as a husband—after she'd told him about the baby, of course. Not only would the baby have a father, but

Abby would have a kind, generous and reliable husband she could count on.

JEFF WAITED AT THE ENTRANCE to Abby's condo building, a shining red sports car behind him. If she wouldn't come with him willingly, he'd simply kidnap her. One way or another, they were going to talk.

He'd only met Abby a few times before today. Each time she'd appeared lovelier. And each time she'd become a different person. She'd gone from being Scarlett O'Malley, a heart-stopping sensual woman and lover, to a sedate businesswoman, and back to a desirable woman. Today, she came out of her building dressed casually: her hair was tied back and she wore loose-fitting khakis that made her look as if she was ready for an adventure.

Her bright blue linen jacket open over a turtleneck sweater deepened the color of her sparkling blue-green eyes. The sweater revealed just enough of her charms to send a man's thoughts along paths that Jeff decided were better not traveled at the moment.

He didn't know where Abby was headed, but she was dressed perfectly for the afternoon he had planned for them.

Her look of surprise when she noticed him pleased him. Caught off guard, she was surely more likely to go along with him without an argument.

"Taking the day off, are you?"

She glanced down the rain-swept street for a moment. "I was planning on taking a walk before changing and going in to work."

"How about taking the day off and coming up to Santa Barbara with me?" he coaxed. "I need to check out a hotel up the coast that the corporation is thinking of buying. I could use your opinion."

To his satisfaction, it took all of three minutes for her to agree.

Heck, kidnapping Abby was easier than he'd thought it was going to be. Lost in admiration of the surprisingly uncharacteristic khakis that hugged Abby's delectable rear, Jeff held the car door open for her. Too old for him, she'd said? No way. As far as he was concerned, any woman would be lucky to look like her.

In that moment, she became his Scarlett again. He stifled a sexual excitement at the thought. His mission for the day was to show her how to lighten up and enjoy life. To get to know her. To have her get to know him. And to show her that she was as young as she wanted to be. And then...

He closed the car door behind Abby, walked around to the other side, and slid into the driver's seat.

"Just friends, remember?" she said when she caught his smile.

"Sure, friends," he answered lightly. He hid the smile. Confident that nature would eventually take its course, he hadn't exactly promised.

He was willing to bet a bundle that underneath that composed exterior beat a heart as warm as the

Acapulco sun. The thought sent his blood racing.
With a cautionary check behind him, he set the car
in gear and shot away from the curb.

In minutes, he saw a frown pass over Abby's forehead. "Second thoughts?"

"I'm not so sure this is a good idea, after all,"
Abby answered. "I did have a few return calls to
make."

"You can make them tomorrow. Think of today
as a holiday. Just sit back and leave everything to
me." He patted her on her knee.

Abby didn't looked convinced. Jeff remembered
she'd mentioned the only time she'd allowed herself
to be completely carefree had been the night she'd
spent in Acapulco with him. And she'd had to run
away from home to accomplish it.

"Relax, Abby," he said. "Put yourself in my
hands. I'm going to show you that you don't need
to run away to Mexico, or anywhere else, to have
fun. Or, if you feel like running again, run to me."

He meant it when he'd told Abby to leave everything to him. But what she didn't know was that
he'd meant more than the ride up to Santa Barbara
and back. He wanted to show her how much she
was beginning to mean to him. And to find out how
much he meant to her.

Abby relaxed against the back of the seat. If the
day didn't shape up as she'd intended, at least it
would give her a chance to get the fresh air and light
exercise that her doctor had recommended. And,
more importantly, a chance to get to know more

about Jeff. She'd already found him to be passionate, intelligent, warm and imaginative—almost too good to be true. Now she had to find out what kind of man he was under that irresistible exterior.

Glancing over at him, a man who made her senses spin, Abby had visions of a younger version of Jeff: a tiny boy or girl with golden-brown hair and sparkling brandy-colored eyes. A killer smile like their father's; a sexy, affectionate man who intuitively seemed to know how to get her attention.

Seated too close to him for comfort, Abby tugged at the neckline of her sweater and glanced over at her companion. He had a secret smile on his face and was whistling softly to the music coming from the car radio.

Actually, his carefree presence was one of the things that had attracted her to him. That and his magnetic smile. He'd made her feel as if she were the only woman on the planet and the one destined to share a lifetime with him. And, to her growing awareness, she felt that way again.

She caught his sidelong glance.

"Awfully quiet, aren't you?" he asked. "Something on your mind?"

"Actually, I was wondering if we were going to stop to eat," she alibied, too embarrassed to share her thoughts with him.

He smiled. "I thought ahead and had the hotel pack a picnic lunch."

Lunch. Abby silently tested the effect the word had on her stomach. To her relief, all was well.

"Good," she answered, "I'm starved. When do we eat?"

Jeff burst into laughter. "Now you sound just like me and my sister Elaine. Whenever Dad took us along with him—not that he did it very often—we drove him nuts with questions. 'How far is it?' 'When can we stop to eat?' And more of the same. My mother kept insisting on those rides because they'd bond us together as a family, but it didn't take. The rides stopped as soon as he could get out of taking us. I guess you could say Dad's not the fatherly type—not then and not now."

Abby caught the wistful expression that crossed his face. "You miss not having a closer relationship with your family, don't you?"

"Yes," he answered simply.

They cruised north along Highway 1, the scenic route that snaked its way northward along the California coast. Below them, the ocean sparkled as the spring sun made its appearance from behind a cloud.

They came to Ventura, then turned right at a sign pointing to Ojai, a small town nestled in a verdant valley surrounded by low hills. They passed through fruit orchards and orange groves, the trees starting to blossom now that spring was here. She inhaled the scent of freshly turned earth and orange blossoms and turned her thoughts to more pleasant subjects.

"Still hungry?"

Abby nodded. So far, so good. "Very."

"It's almost noon. We'll have lunch in a few

minutes.'' He headed left at a sign pointing to Matillja Hot Springs and a few minutes later pulled to a stop on a bluff overlooking a flowing creek.

Abby gazed around her at the green hills on the other side of the road, the ancient oak trees that dotted the landscape. In the background, she could hear the sound of running water, of mating birds calling to one another. The surroundings were beautiful, but she was too hungry to appreciate them at the moment.

"A picnic here? Are you sure you're in the right place?"

"As sure as my name is— Never mind," he added with a wry grin. "Just follow me. You'll have to climb down the embankment to a stream below here, so be careful. I'll go ahead to make sure the trail is clear."

While Abby watched, he disappeared from sight, and leery of being left alone on the deserted road, she started after him. Sliding down the slope, she found herself squarely in his arms.

He held her so closely that she felt the pressure of his hips against hers. His instant arousal as he caught her in his arms heightened her own awareness of him. She wanted to kiss him, taste him, touch him, hear him whisper his desire for her. To share what they'd shared on a deserted Acapulco beach.

Lips hard with passion pressed against hers, urged hers to open to him. Instinctively, she responded. The taste of him, the feel of his hard body against hers, was almost more than she could bear. They were reactions she'd never intended to have again, but she couldn't control them.

Friends, Abby thought dimly. How foolish to have thought she could dismiss the way she felt about him, let alone dismiss the way he obviously felt about her.

A moment later, Jeff lifted his head, took a deep breath and gazed down at her. "Sorry, I didn't intend for that to happen. It's just that whenever I get close to you, I want to hold you in my arms. I'm afraid one thing leads to another," he said ruefully.

Abby leaned against his solid strength and waited for her desire to ebb. If ever there was a time to turn away from his charisma, it was now. Now, before he misunderstood the direction of their future relationship. "I suppose you're right. The question is, should it?"

"Why not?" he said playfully, brushing her hair away from her eyes. "Give me one good reason."

"I told you before," she answered. "We're two different people from two different worlds. You need someone your own age and background to play with."

"I'd much rather have you as a playmate," he answered, lowering his lips to hers again. His soft, full voice mesmerized her. When he outlined her lips with his tongue, common sense surrendered to desire.

"You're not going to run away from me this time, are you, Scarlett?"

Scarlett! The nickname was a reminder of the

night when she'd shed her Abby Carson persona and become Scarlett O'Malley—a woman without responsibilities who could live for the moment.

But things were different now. She had a precious new life to consider, and a future full of uncertainties.

She fought her way to the surface of the whirlpool. "I don't think this is exactly what 'friendship' means, do you?" she murmured.

He blinked as if she'd thrown cold water over him. "Friendship? If this isn't being friendly," he said nuzzling her cheek, "I don't know what friendship is."

"You did promise me lunch?" she said when she could catch her breath. "I really am starved."

He sighed and let her go. "You don't make it easy on a guy, do you?" he said with a shaky laugh. "Lunch, it is." He rose in one fluid motion. "I have to go back to the car for the picnic hamper, but I'll be back in a minute."

When Jeff returned, he spread a blanket under the tree and unpacked the hamper. Abby eyed a few interested ants warily, but she was starved and willing to fight for her lunch.

"Tell me more about your father," Abby finally asked as she munched on an apple. She needed to know more about Jeff, the family man. She felt she already knew the playboy.

He looked bewildered at the topic but gave in with a shrug. "What's to tell?"

"Rumor has it your father wants you to take over the Logan hotels."

"Partly true. Only the Logan Wilshire, actually. Dad sees it as a trial balloon."

"And you don't agree?"

"Hardly," he shrugged. "Too bad he can't see my sister Elaine is the one who should take over when he's ready to retire. She's worked in various management positions at the corporate offices in San Francisco for several years. Knows more about the business than anyone else except Dad."

"Instead, he wants you?"

"Don't know why," he answered. "We've never seen eye to eye. It isn't that I haven't tried—I've worked hard for the corporation for seven years. It's just that my interests lie in a different direction." His glance was rueful. "I just want to write."

No one's life was perfect, Abby mused as she caught a glimpse of the real man behind the quirky grin. Not even Jeff's. At the beginning, she'd thought he was a wealthy playboy, a man who had everything, including choices. Now that she caught a glimpse of the man behind the surface, it appeared that his wealthy background had given him neither happiness nor a real family.

That was another problem, Abby decided as she added the problem of his indecision about his future to the difference in their ages. He was like Richard, her ex-husband, wandering through life in pursuit of a dream. Still, seeing the faraway dream in Jeff's eyes, watching changing emotions cross his face, and hearing the regret in his voice as he spoke of his relationship with his father, she realized he could easily be a man she could fall in love with.

"Turnabout is fair play," Jeff said. "Tell me, what is it that makes Abby run?"

"Run?"

Jeff reached to idly finger a golden strand of her hair that had fallen over her eyes. "You are thinking of running away from me, aren't you?"

Abby hesitated. How could she tell him the truth without hurting him? How could she tell him that she didn't feel secure with him—not when he couldn't make up his mind about his future? "Being practical isn't exactly running away," she finally answered. "From the time I married and then divorced Richard, I've spent most of my life being responsible for someone else. I've worked hard to get where I am. I still have Kate and my mother depending on me. Now that I've earned security for them, I can't see myself being selfish and throwing it away for a brief fling. Even a pleasurable one."

"A fling? Is that all I mean to you?"

The hurt in Jeff's eyes cracked her resolve to keep their relationship platonic.

"No," she answered with a soft smile. "I admit, I do care a lot about you. But that doesn't change anything," she added when he reached for her. "I have a safe and sane future to think about."

"Safe and sane," he echoed. "That's the old Abby talking." He shook his head, rose and drew her to her feet. "Scarlett, I do believe you're in for a surprise."

At the look in his eyes, Abby stirred uneasily. This was to have been a simple outing. His eyes said something more. "I thought you said we had a hotel to look at."

"It's not very far from here. We have plenty of time," he answered as he bent to kiss her.

Abby hesitated. She didn't want to contemplate what could happen next if they didn't move on. Her good intentions would undoubtedly be shot to pieces. They had enough holes in them already.

"We can't stay here."

"Why not?"

"I've already told you. I can't afford to fall in love with you. You just don't want to listen." She shook her head, struggled to her feet and started to make her way up the slope to the car. Behind her, she heard him sigh, gather the blanket and the picnic hamper, and start up the slope behind her.

She realized Jeff cared for her in his own way. But it wasn't *her* way. Their backgrounds and their ages weren't the only things that stood between them. Soon, there would be the baby.

Abby couldn't deny that Jeff was honest, well-intentioned, and attractive to the point of distraction.

But was he the man she could trust with her heart—and her child's future?

Chapter Five

Abby was grateful for Jeff's silence as they continued up the coastal highway. Reason told her she was right. What they had between them could be nothing more than infatuation. Too bad her heart told another story.

Except for the time of her divorce from Richard, she couldn't remember a time when she'd been filled with such indecision. When the split had finally come, they'd both agreed they'd married too young. They had drifted apart for several years before their divorce, but, in some strange way, they actually still loved each other.

Now there was Jeff, with the same charm, the same faraway dream in his eyes as her former husband. Like Richard, Jeff was easy to love. But, like a younger Richard, he still wasn't able to reconcile his dreams with reality.

Abby sighed. The baby she was carrying was reality. Maybe even more reality than Jeff could face at this stage of his life.

"We're almost there," Jeff announced. He turned

into a side road that disappeared into the distance. A sign pointed the way to Rancho Del Ciel. Ten minutes later, they drew up in front of a two-story, early-California ranch house that had been converted into a hotel.

Nestled high in the hills above the Pacific Ocean, the white-and-brown building with its wide veranda was surrounded by brightly colored masses of wisteria vines, spring flowers and jasmine bushes. Ancient oak trees stood guard over the house. A water fountain played in the courtyard. In the background, half hidden by verdant foliage, Abby could see a dozen small cottages.

She was impressed. "This is a hotel?"

"More than a hotel," Jeff answered with a grin. "It's another slice of paradise."

Another slice of paradise. Abby's heart skipped.

Jeff came around to her side and opened the car door for her. "Come with me. I'd like to show you something." He led her along a path around the back of the ranch house and down a meandering trail leading to the cottage area. "Beautiful, isn't it?"

"I can't believe anyone would be willing to let this place go," Abby said as she admired the vintage building and its surrounding scenery. "If it were mine, I'd never let it go." She drew in a deep breath and inhaled the scent of the early spring wildflowers that bloomed in haphazard clumps as if nature hadn't been sure where to drop the seeds.

"Luckily for us, someone is willing to sell. The

Logan Corporation is considering taking an option to buy it.''

"Tell them to close the deal as fast as they can," Abby commented. "A hotel like this comes along once in a lifetime. Look over there. You can actually see the Pacific Ocean over the horizon."

He came to a stop in front of one of the more remote cottages. "This is something I especially wanted you to see."

Abby gazed at the small wooden building. It resembled a large Victorian dollhouse complete with gables, gingerbread trim and lace curtains at the windows. But what made her heart beat faster was the wall of flowering red hibiscus bushes that were entwined in the latticework trim. The same flower that had covered the hotel grounds in Mexico.

"You had to have been here before today to know about this cottage," she said slowly, looking up into his eyes. "When?"

"The day after we went shopping for a place of my own. The minute I saw it, I knew you'd love it."

So Jeff had planned today's visit. Wanting her opinion had been an excuse. "You've already decided to recommend buying the ranch, haven't you?"

"To be truthful, yes," he answered, stilling her protest with a gentle finger on her lips. "I used that as a reason to get you to come up here with me. I wasn't sure you would be willing to say 'yes' otherwise."

"What made you think I wouldn't go for a ride with you this afternoon?"

"Maybe because of all that talk about being friends?"

The man was crazy, all right, Abby mused. Crazy like a fox. She'd gone with him on a sudden impulse, not really knowing why, or what to expect. Knowing only that at the moment he'd represented a time in her life that she was somehow reluctant to let go.

She *was* attracted to him, despite her practical side warning her that the path ahead was bound to be rocky. So much so that her earlier suggestion they remain just friends had been more of a defensive measure than a proposal. "So, why did you really bring me here?"

"Simple. I told you, I thought you might enjoy seeing the cottage and its surroundings. You do like it, don't you?"

Abby studied him for a long moment. She felt that she already knew enough about him to recognize his studied innocence. "That's all? You wanted me to see a cottage?"

"Why? What else did you think I had in mind?"

She blushed under his scrutiny.

"I'm sure I could think of something else if you're willing," he said, tweaking a tendril away from her rosy cheek. He sensed it wouldn't be difficult, not when Abby was every bit as lovely as she'd been the first time he'd noticed her on the

hotel terrace. She'd never been far from his mind
and his thoughts ever since.

"Wait a minute," she said. "I thought we'd
agreed to be friends."

"*You* agreed," he answered. "*I'm* still thinking
about it." He reached over her shoulder, plucked
two red blossoms from a hibiscus bush and offered
her one. "This looks familiar, doesn't it?" When
she nodded, he regarded her with a broad smile.
"Actually, I think we do have something in common."

The night in Acapulco with all its vivid memories
rushed into Abby's mind as she gazed at the vivid
red flower that he held out to her. He *had* remembered the flowering hibiscus bushes on the hotel
grounds. She *had* been more than a night's pleasure
to him. She felt her eyes mist with happiness.

Still, she had to make one more attempt to reason
with him—with herself.

"I'm pleased you remembered," she told him.
"But I'd still like to remain just friends."

"Agreed," he answered with that lopsided smile
that shook her down to her toes, "but maybe friends
don't have to be merely friends all the time."

"This isn't what I had in mind when I agreed
to..." Her voice trailed away. How was she ever
going to be able to resist this man when his sensuous
glance and velvet voice suggested there could be
more than mere friendship between them?

He tucked a flower behind her ear. "In Hawaii,

if a woman wears a hibiscus flower behind her left ear, it means she's available.''

"And when she wears the flower behind her right ear?" Abby asked, mesmerized.

"It means she's taken."

Silently, she took the flower from her left ear and put it behind her right. Not because she wanted to, but because she had to somehow show him she'd been serious when she'd tried to draw a line between friendship and something more intimate.

"That's all right with me, too," he said with that same magical smile that never failed to touch her heart. "Either way, I'd like to believe the message is meant for me."

Abby laughed at the way Jeff could turn anything around. "I don't know what I'm going to do with you," she said helplessly. "I've never met anyone with such a one-track mind."

Jeff was surprised at his mind-set, too. Until he'd met Abby, he'd never cared enough about any one woman to want to form a lasting relationship. In Abby's case, he'd discovered her attraction was more than physical. She was intelligent and funny. She listened to him, and, unlike most of the women he'd been introduced to, she made him feel that she saw him as a person—apart from his background and wealth. He felt so comfortable around Abby; he'd managed to tell her more in a few hours about himself than he'd ever said aloud to another living soul, except his sister. And, maybe even more.

He began to see today's Abby differently from

the woman he'd met in Mexico. He admired her for the firm head on her lovely shoulders. And for her pragmatic views that had taken her through a life that couldn't have been a bed of roses. As far as having fun, he had to admit "fun" obviously meant different things to different people.

Who was he to decide how Abby should live her life? Especially when he still didn't know how he wanted to spend his. Gazing down into the depths of her enchanting blue-green eyes, he knew he wanted more than friendship from her.

He wanted more of her than just a few companionable hours spent admiring the landscape together. More of holding her in his arms. He couldn't let her go without at least trying to show her how much he cared for her. How much he wanted her.

"Abby," he said impulsively, "let's spend the night here."

"Here? Tonight? In this cottage?"

"Why not? I looked inside the last time I was here. I'm sure you'll love it," he went on. "There's a living room with a sleeper sofa and a real fireplace. And in the other room, there's a bedroom with a queen-size bed."

Maybe he shouldn't have mentioned the bed, he realized when he saw Abby's eyes narrow. She was no dummy; she no doubt suspected what he had on his mind. He changed it fast. "You can have the bed. I'll take the sofa."

"I don't know," she answered, drawing her arms

around her. "It sounds lovely, but I'm not sure if it's wise for us to spend the night together."

He tried again. "If you get hungry, there's a five-star restaurant. And if you'd rather not go out, we could order room service."

Abby tried to resist the hunger in his eyes. She tried to be practical, to remember the reasons why she shouldn't spend the night with him. To give him credit, after seeing the earnest look on his face and hearing his offer to sleep on the sofa, she couldn't think of one.

Taken by the yearning in his voice, she felt herself responding to the hunger she felt for him. After all, she reasoned, she had nothing to lose, and maybe a different kind of memory to gain.

"I can tell you're exhausted, Abby. If we stay, you can get a good night's rest," he coaxed. "We could go horseback riding in the morning, and swim in the hotel's heated pool afterwards."

Horseback riding? Abby couldn't even recall the last time she'd been on a horse. Plus, she was sure horseback riding was not recommended for expectant mothers in their first trimester. And as for getting a good night's rest... With Jeff in the next room, she had her doubts about that, too.

"No, thanks, I've never gone horseback riding," she answered, deciding to play it safe. Better to say "no" outright than to face explanations. "I don't think so."

"No to the horseback riding, or to spending the night here with me?"

Abby wanted to say "both," but the magic of the brilliant red-and-yellow breaking sunset and the man asking the question were too hard to resist.

As her gaze locked with his, Abby's senses clamored for her to say "yes." His eyes were warm pools that drew her into their depths, made her ache with the need to be held, to be loved again as only he could love her. To make up for all the lonely years behind her.

She struggled for an answer. She'd never met a man who made her feel so wanted, so needed, so feminine. In Jeff's gaze, she saw herself as a desired woman.

She slowly took the red flower from her right ear and replaced it behind the left. At the signal, a broad smile came over his face. "Yes, I'll stay."

"I'm glad you didn't say 'no,' or try to run away the way you did in Mexico," he said, grabbing her around her waist and twirling in a circle with her until she was breathless. "Because," he added, "if you ever feel like running away from anything again, remember what I told you. I hope you'll want to run to me."

Jeff's words seemed to reach in and tug at her heart. She longed to do just as he asked, to run to him and never leave again. But her mind would not let her heart make that choice. "Clothes," she managed to say. "I don't have a change of clothing with me. I don't even have a toothbrush or a nightgown."

"Don't worry," Jeff assured her. "There's a gift shop up at the main house. Let's go and see if the cottage is available for tonight. If it is, you can shop while I register. Pick up anything you need and charge it to the room. And, as for a nightgown..." His voice trailed off, a smile hovered at his lips.

Abby remembered the last time they'd spent the night together. A night under tropical skies when the only thing that had covered her had been Jeff's shirt. And then, only after he'd made passionate love to her.

Abby felt as if her body temperature had risen by ten degrees. She couldn't answer him. Some memories were made to be cherished. This was one she couldn't bring herself to speak about openly.

"I have to make a telephone call first. Then I'll go shopping," she told him firmly. "You don't have to pay for anything."

"Come on, Abby. From what I hear from Nadine, you're always doing something nice for someone else. Why can't you let me do something for you?"

"You already have," Abby answered, keeping herself from touching her stomach.

Now that the first shock of finding herself pregnant had worn off, Abby didn't regret the baby. Maybe because Kate had been an only child and because she hadn't had the chance to enjoy Kate's childhood as much as she would have liked to. Now that she had the time, income and maturity to do it right, she intended to enjoy this baby.

The fact that Jeffrey was the baby's biological father somehow pleased her, she mused as she glanced at his solid profile. If only he were a little older and had settled down to a career...

She headed for the nearest pay phone.

"Kate, this is your mother. I've decided to spend the night in Santa Barbara. I'll see you tomorrow." Abby could hardly believe she was saying the words.

"Mother, wait a minute. Sebastian wanted to talk to you!" Kate sounded almost frantic.

Abby sighed. Sebastian was unfinished business. A business she wasn't in a hurry to resolve. "Tell him I'll see him tomorrow night. And don't forget to tell your grandmother I won't be home tonight."

Abby escaped the telephone call with a promise to come home as early as possible. She purchased her toiletries and, with deliberation, an extra-large T-shirt to wear as a nightgown.

"Ready, Abby?"

Thank goodness he'd given up calling her Scarlett, Abby thought as she put her change in her wallet. The less attention he drew to them, the better.

Inside, the cottage lived up to everything Jeff had promised. Vases of fresh-cut flowers were scattered around the sitting room. A welcome basket of apples, pears and wrapped chocolate kisses waited on the bar. A quick glance revealed a small kitchen area with a refrigerator.

"Where can I leave my things?"

"Over in here," Jeff answered. He slid open the accordion doors that shielded the bedroom area.

Abby followed him and dropped her packages on

a pine chest at the foot of an antique four-poster bed. Covered with a handmade quilt, the bed occupied the center of the room. The scent of lilac potpourri filled the air. Enough logs and kindling were stacked in a large brass basket alongside the fireplace to ward off the chill of spring nights.

"It looks like a page out of *The Little House on the Prairie* TV show, doesn't it?"

"Only better," Jeff replied, shrugging off his coat.

"Better?" Abby lovingly smoothed the rose-and-green quilt where Jeff had tossed his jacket.

"Yes, because you're here."

Another little piece of Abby's resolve to keep her emotional distance melted. If he kept this up, she was afraid they were rapidly going to move beyond her definition of "friendship." She shook her head. "I don't know what I'm going to do with you if you keep saying romantic things like that."

"Me, romantic? Hardly." He laughed. "I was just telling it like it is."

Abby turned away to hide a smile. "How about dinner?"

Jeff glanced around the room and, with a wry smile, put on his jacket.

She liked knowing that he wasn't aware of his own sensuality. And that he hadn't originally planned ahead on spending the night. In fact, she thought as she followed him outside and waited while he locked the cottage door, if he were any more romantic, she'd pull him back inside the cottage and throw away the key.

The dining room decor resembled a wine cellar built into the foot of the slope at the back of the main ranch house. A violinist played in the background as they entered. She smiled and followed the headwaiter to a secluded corner.

"A glass of wine for the lady?"

Abby shook her head. "Ginger ale, please, with extra ice."

"I'll have a margarita, with extra lime," Jeff added. She avoided his puzzled glance.

When the waiter left, Jeff studied Abby. "Glad you decided to stay?"

"Very," she answered. "Tell me more about the story you're writing," she said while they waited to be served.

"There's not much to tell," he answered with a smile. "Like all stories, and life itself, it has a beginning, a middle and an end. And—since it's a romantic suspense—a happy one."

His thoughtful expression as he gazed at her made Abby wonder about the meaning behind his answer. If he meant their story, theirs certainly had had a memorable beginning. Now that they were living the middle of the story, if she told him about the outcome of that encounter, how would that affect the end?

She toyed with her salad and turned her thoughts to the night ahead and Jeff's offer to sleep on the sofa bed. Recalling the glint in his eyes when he made the offer, she shivered.

"Dessert, madame?"

"No, thank you," she answered. "I have to watch my weight." It was true. Beth had cautioned her not to gain more than twenty or twenty-five pounds.

"Thank you, we'll both pass," Jeff told the waiter who'd handed him the dessert menu. He thought longingly of hot apple pie topped with ice cream, but it didn't seem fair to tempt Abby when she was dieting.

Abby wasn't exactly thin, but as far as he was concerned she was perfect. He gazed at her, visualizing her in the tempting black slip dress, and the lace-trimmed teddy she'd worn underneath, before he'd dared her to join him in the midnight-blue waters of Acapulco Bay.

She'd tried to cover the more strategic parts of her body that night, he recalled, but enough of her porcelain flesh had been revealed to him in all its glorious detail.

For his sanity's sake, Jeff reined his thoughts. He tried to make small talk. It wasn't easy.

Dinner over, they silently walked back to the cottage. He took her hand. She let him. The moon cast its magical glow over the hotel grounds; the scent of jasmine filled the air. Inside the cottage, a low fire was glowing in the bedroom fireplace, courtesy of the tip he'd slipped a grateful bellman.

Abby yawned. "I can't understand why I'm so sleepy."

She did look beat. "Tell you what," he said sympathetically as he helped her remove her jacket. "Why don't you get comfortable, while I lock up and make a few telephone calls?"

Abby nodded and headed for the bedroom.

She was wearing an oversize T-shirt, her hair in a ponytail, and looked ready for bed, when Jeff came back into the bedroom.

"Here, let me help you," he said, trying to ignore his reaction to the way Abby looked tonight. She looked young and vulnerable and trusting, all in one appealing package. He swallowed his comments, took the throw pillows off the bed and threw back the covers.

"Jeff—"

"Just trying to help, that's all. Honest."

The look on his face amused Abby, but she was too tired to comment. Smothering a laugh, she slid into bed. "Good night," she said sleepily. "See you in the morning."

Jeff groaned. He had hoped for more, but a promise was a promise. By the time he'd turned off the lamps, he saw a soft smile on Abby's face, as though she was dreaming of something that made her happy. He wanted to believe she was dreaming of the two of them on warm, tropical sands.

He shrugged philosophically. Proud of himself for his restraint, he went into the bathroom to shower and undress. Abby's sheer lacy undergarments were hanging behind the shower curtain—an exquisite reminder of the woman asleep in the next room.

Enough to make a grown man ache for what he couldn't have. He hung the garments on a towel rack, showered and reluctantly made for the sofa bed and the long night ahead.

ABBY STIRRED AND AWAKENED to find a decidedly masculine arm thrown across her middle. *Impossible,* she thought. She'd gone to bed alone. She cautiously turned her head and warily followed the arm to a bare, masculine shoulder—Jeff's!

Shocked, she lay quietly while she tried to recall what had happened last night before she went to sleep.

Laundry. She'd washed her underwear and hung it behind the shower curtain. What in heaven's name had she been thinking of? she wondered when the fresh scent of soap on Jeff's skin told her he had also showered before going to bed. A flush ran through her when she visualized what his reaction must have been when he'd found her underwear.

She glanced at the rumpled sofa bed in the next room. If he'd actually gone to sleep there last night, what was he doing here in bed beside her this morning?

She was sure of one thing: they hadn't made love last night, or her body would have told her.

She glanced over at Jeff. The blanket had slipped down far enough for her to see every detail of his tanned, bare torso. He was fast asleep. Golden-brown eyelashes lay across his cheeks. His breathing was warm and measured.

Abby felt tempted by his warmth, *too* tempted...
She'd better be up and dressed before he awakened,
or she wouldn't be getting out of bed any time soon.
She bent over to make sure he was asleep, then gingerly started to slide from under the arm that held
her.

Too late. Jeff opened his eyes. Sure enough, and
just as she'd feared, temptation stared back at her.

"Please don't move," he murmured sleepily.
"You're just where I want you to be."

Just where he wanted her to be! Typical male,
Abby thought with an inward smile, even while she
realized that she liked being where he wanted her to
be.

"What are you doing here? I thought we'd agreed
you'd take the sofa?"

"I did, and I kept my word," he said. "Until I
heard you call me in your sleep. I figured if I joined
you, you'd settle down and get a good night's rest."
He gestured to his jeans. "I even put these on so
you wouldn't get the wrong idea, in case you woke
up before I did."

Abby smiled feebly. What in heaven's name had
she said in her sleep last night? Had she said something that she might live to regret? Or, worse yet,
had she given away her secret about the baby? She
couldn't bring herself to ask.

As for Jeff, if he didn't want her to get the wrong
idea about what had happened during the night, it
was too late. Jeans or not, his nude torso was enough

to give her a number of ideas. None of which she could afford to pursue.

"Feeling better, Abby? You were pretty sacked out last night."

"I thought I did." Abby smothered a yawn. "I can't seem to get enough sleep lately."

"You must have needed the rest." His gaze rested on her bare shoulder where the T-shirt had slid down.

Abby instinctively reached for cover. She wasn't showing yet, but last night in the bathroom mirror, she'd noticed a number of changes in her body. A fullness to her breasts, a slight, barely noticeable bulge to her stomach.

"You fell asleep so fast, I didn't even get a chance to say good-night properly."

Abby's antenna picked up a sultry nuance in his voice. Her hormones snapped to attention. He'd opened the door to something...more than a mere discussion of what was a proper good-night. She stared at him blankly, aware of every inch of him. And of herself. *Now* what?

Chapter Six

"Properly?" Abby echoed, almost afraid, yet eager in spite of herself to find out just what "properly" entailed.

"Yes, properly." He reached up, cupped her face with his warm hands and drew her down to him. "Like this." His kiss landed on her forehead. He moved down her cheek. By the time he reached her lips, she was a molten mass of desire.

He murmured softly and, when she didn't resist, moved on to her neck where a vein throbbed. With a sigh, and a final hug, he finally let her go.

Instinct warned Abby to move. There had to be a safer place than beside a half-nude man. A man who melted her with a touch, a kiss. Not that she felt dressed, either. The T-shirt, once long enough to reach her knees, threatened to move up north with every move she made.

"That was a good-night kiss for last night," Jeff told her, drawing back. He flashed her that quirky smile she loved, and Abby knew she didn't stand a chance. "Now, it's time for a good-morning kiss."

His morning kisses took on a greater urgency and, in moments, elicited a not-too-unexpected reaction. Her body felt like dry timber, and his kisses the approaching fire.

"I have to get up," Abby said faintly. She squirmed in his arms, trying to pull the T-shirt down to safer territory. "I promised Kate I'd come home early."

"She can wait a few hours. This is more important."

"It's not only Kate," Abby said breathlessly, giving up on the T-shirt. "She told me Sebastian wants to talk to me."

"Later," he said, drawing her back and nuzzling the tender spot under her chin. "I enjoy waking up with you in the morning too much to let you get away from me so soon."

Abby gazed into Jeff's bemused smile. In spite of the sexy suggestions and the sensuous invitation in his voice, he was clearly waiting for her to make the next move. Choices raged through her mind.

Reason told her to leave.

Desire held her still.

With a groan that carried with it all the sexual frustration he must have felt, Jeff released her. "If you really want to leave now, Abby, we will. But say it now, while I can still let you go."

She knew that she should have asked to leave, but something held her back. Wasn't this subconsciously why she'd agreed to spend the night with him? What purpose would it serve to deny herself, and him, the fulfillment of that desire?

When she hesitated, Jeff's lips settled on hers— but only for a moment. "Wait a minute, Abby," Jeff muttered, drawing back to catch his breath. "I honestly didn't plan this. I don't know any other way to tell you, but I'm afraid I didn't bring anything with me. Do you need protection?"

Abby shook her head. How could she tell him that he was almost three months too late?

Jeff breathed a sigh of relief at her silence. Luckily, he'd had protection with him the night he'd met Abby for the first time. Not that he'd planned the interlude that had followed. Shielding her from unwanted attentions that night had been a reflex action on his part. Asking her to walk with him in moonlit gardens had been a spur-of-the-moment impulse. The rest of the night had become the most incredible of his life. Awakening the following morning to find himself alone had been the most frustrating of his life.

Now that he'd found Abby again, he ached to make love to her, to drown in her soft, golden beauty. But the last thing he wanted to do was to put her in any kind of jeopardy.

He understood her silence. Even after the wonderful night they'd spent in Mexico, Jeff realized that for a woman like Abby the decision to make love wouldn't come lightly.

If she stood a chance of becoming pregnant without protection tonight, surely she would tell him so.

Maybe she was too embarrassed to tell him it was that time in her cycle when she couldn't get pregnant.

His eyes locked with hers. When he saw indecision cross her face, he schooled himself to hold back, to wait until she showed him that she wanted him as much as he wanted her.

He was tempted to try to persuade her. To caress her until she was ready to let him wrap himself around her, to make love to her until she forgot everything but the two of them and the way they felt about each other. But he cared about her too much to insist.

Abby gazed at him with an uncertain smile. "In spite of what you might think, I don't usually..." she began.

"You don't have to convince me, Abby," he answered. "I sensed that about you almost from the first moment we met. It was one of the special things I remembered about you, and one of the reasons I'd hoped to find you again. You might have been married before, but you have a refreshing, uncalculated charm that I connect with. And you're so darn honest, it actually hurts," he added wryly. "In more ways than one."

"I'm sorry." She colored as she answered. "I've never meant to lead you on, or to hurt you."

"It's not your fault, Abby," he added. "To tell the truth, I wanted to make love to you again from the moment I saw you at the banquet. You may not realize it, but you're so easy to love," he teased.

"Thank you."

She placed a gentle finger against his lips. "Now, enough talk."

Jeff didn't need a second invitation. He rose to his knees and brought Abby with him. He gathered the hem of her T-shirt in his hands and slowly, inch by inch—stopping only long enough to place kisses over her rosy skin as it was exposed to him—he slid the shirt up over her middle, her breasts. Her warm skin was rosy, and he wanted to believe it was because she desired him.

He sat back on his heels, the better to admire the lovely body of the woman whose face and figure he'd never forgotten.

"Tell me what you like, Abby," he murmured. "I want to make love to you in ways you'll never forget."

"Only you," she whispered. "Only you." She drew the T-shirt off her shoulders and tossed it over the side of the bed.

It was all the encouragement Jeff needed. He pulled off the slacks that bound him, releasing the desire that pulsated underneath. With a low groan, he took her into his arms.

He could feel the rapid beat of her heart as her lush breasts pressed against his heated skin. He trailed kisses down the velvety skin of her throat and reveled in her soft murmurs of pleasure when his fingers found and teased her breasts.

As Abby responded to his lovemaking with a passion that matched his own, she became the wonderfully sensuous woman he remembered. In his arms, she became a mixture of all things feminine, womanly. And, in the first rays of daylight breaking through the lace curtains at the bedroom windows, she looked more desirable than ever.

"Abby," he murmured into her throat. "Now that I've found you again, I'm never going to let you go."

He heard her catch her breath. He thought she was going to protest. Instead, she kissed him with an urgency that heightened the passion surging through him. To his delight, in his arms the pragmatic Abby Carson who wanted to remain friends disappeared and became the wild and sensuous Scarlett O'Malley.

In the eyes that burned her with their passion, Abby saw the heat of Jeff's desire for her. She tasted it on his lips, felt it on his tongue as he traced the line of her jaw and kissed the hollow between her breasts. She shivered with pleasure when he ran his hands over the parts of her body that had become more sensitive than she'd realized.

When his strong, sleek and heated body finally covered hers and made her his, Abby felt herself pulled under turbulent wave after wave of sensation. Sensation that carried her across an erotic sea down into shimmering depths before she rose to the surface where waves crashed around her.

She realized in those few moments that she'd captured the excitement and sense of sexual adventure she'd missed so much of her adult life. Fulfilled as never before, she could scarcely believe this could happen to her at this time in her life.

In the arms that held her, Abby felt she had become the woman she'd longed to be in her more uninhibited moments. Only Jeff could have made those fantasies come true, she thought as he tongued her damp and salty skin.

Maybe this was wrong. Maybe they didn't belong together. But, somehow, the here and now were all that mattered.

"Abby?" Jeff soothed her aching lips with a gentle touch of his forefinger. "You're awfully quiet. What are you thinking about?"

"Nothing important," she answered, returning Jeff's smoky gaze. Perspiration clung to his slick muscular chest; the lock of hair that perpetually fell over his forehead hung over smiling eyes. She touched him, feeling again the firm body of a young man.

She lay back and drew the sheets over her, wondering once again what he thought of her mature figure, years older than his. Sexual euphoria ebbed slowly as she considered the relationship ahead of them. But not the love she knew by now had been building slowly but surely, in spite of her good intentions.

How could she have become so involved with him when she felt he was too young for her? When she knew their backgrounds and their futures were worlds apart?

But how could she deny the sheer magnetism that held her to him?

How could she deny him the right to be a father to his child?

The answers would come sooner or later, she thought. But not now, with Jeff in bed beside her, wearing nothing but a tender smile. Now she couldn't think clearly.

The sunlight that crept into the room revealed the renewed sexual invitation in Jeff's eyes. An answering warmth filled her.

She gathered the last of her willpower and smothered the impulse to slide her hands over Jeff's hot skin, to caress him, to take him to her one more time. If she didn't get dressed and ask to leave now, she knew she would spend the rest of the morning in his arms. With a sigh, she started to retrieve her T-shirt. "I think it's past time to start for home."

"If that's what you really want," he whispered into her throat. "First, I believe we have some unfinished business to take care of."

His devilish smile and the humor dancing in his eyes sent more positive second thoughts racing through Abby as she moved back into his arms.

"HOME AGAIN, DARN IT," Jeff said as they stood hand in hand in front of her condo door. "Maybe I won't let you go in, after all."

Abby laughed as his warm breath tickled her ear. "I have to," she answered. "I promised."

"Promises, promises," he answered. "You've

made all kinds of promises, except the one I want to hear.''

"And which one would that be?" Abby teased, trying to take her hand back so she could reach her keys.

"When we can be together again."

Abby shivered at the mental pictures that came into her mind. "I don't know," she answered over her shoulder. "It all depends on what happens next."

When she unlocked the door to her condo, Kate rushed to meet her.

"Mom! How could you? You said you would be home early and it's almost three o'clock in the afternoon. Sebastian has been waiting for you, and Dad's here."

Abby's sensual afterglow vanished abruptly. The day that had started so full of promise turned dark. She'd known Sebastian would be waiting for her— but Richard?

"Your father's here? Without calling and telling me he's coming?"

"I called him yesterday and he came out right away."

Abby took a deep breath. Something was definitely wrong or Kate wouldn't have called and asked her father to come. As for Richard, it wasn't like him not to call and tell her when to expect him.

She felt the need for moral support, or maybe just a sympathetic ear. From the reproachful tone in Kate's voice, she wasn't quite sure she would find one inside the apartment. She turned back to where Jeff was silently listening.

"Would you like to come inside for a drink?"

"Yes, thank you. A cup of coffee would be great." With a smile at Kate, he followed Abby inside.

The apartment was spacious, filled with soft, sea-foam green and beige upholstered furniture. Here and there, there were touches of brilliant color, as if Abby had chosen to let fly in her decorating scheme her hidden desires. Desires he'd glimpsed only twice. It was as if the reserved Abby Carson was subconsciously competing with the passion of Scarlett O'Malley.

But what bothered him was that he glimpsed a sudden fear in Abby's eyes. A protective feeling for her took root. No one was going to make Abby unhappy if he could help it.

Abby led the way inside. Too late, she realized that the packages in Jeff's arms and on the shopping bag she carried displayed the Rancho Del Ciel Hotel logo. When Kate had enough time to put two and two together, she was bound to realize Abby and Jeff had spent the night together.

She fought her initial panic. After all, Kate was twenty-one and ought to be able to understand her mother spending the night with a man. In any case, Abby wasn't going to let anyone make her ashamed of the way she felt for Jeff. "You've met my daughter, Kate?"

"Yes, of course," Jeff said politely when Kate

was too distracted to do more than nod. "Nice to meet you again."

Abby slipped off her jacket and glanced into the ornate hall mirror. She smoothed away the tendrils that had come loose during Jeff's embrace in the elevator. Her lips looked swollen. Even while she worried that someone would notice, Abby was secretly pleased.

"I'm sorry we're so late," she told Kate. Not strictly true, Abby thought as she led the way inside. How could she be sorry she was late when she felt so well loved? It was just that Kate looked too troubled for comfort. "We were having too good a time to hurry back."

Kate darted a look at Jeff. She glanced away quickly, but Abby noticed a look of surprise cross Kate's face when she must have realized they'd spent the night. One less hurdle to cross, Abby thought with a nervous smile at Jeff.

She walked into the living room. It and the adjoining pristine kitchen were empty. The door to the den was closed. "I thought you said your father and Sebastian were here."

"They're in the den, talking."

"That's nice," Abby answered vaguely. She took her packages from Jeff and dropped them on an upholstered chair together with her shopping bag. "What do you suppose they've found to talk about?"

It seemed to Abby that Kate blushed.

Before Abby could comment, her mother sailed

into the room, her arms filled with her own shopping trophies. "Good, you've finally come home. We were beginning to worry about you." She gave Jeff an uncertain smile. "We have met, haven't we?"

"Yes, we have. At the Realtor's banquet."

"Yes, of course," Abby's mother answered slowly. A broad smile lit up her face. "Now I remember. You're Jeffrey Logan, of the Logan hotels, aren't you?"

"Guilty." Jeff smiled politely. "It's nice to meet you again, Mrs. Baker."

Abby started for the kitchen. "Coffee, Caroline?"

"Yes, thank you." She smiled broadly at Jeff. "What brings you here, young man?"

Abby braced herself for the barrage of questions that were bound to come if she left her mother and Jeff alone. "Why don't you come and help me, Caroline?"

"In a minute," her mother answered as she remained eyeing Jeff. Abby could tell her mother was working up to more than mere pleasantries.

"How have you been, Mr. Logan?"

"Just fine, thank you, Mrs. Baker, but please, call me Jeff."

Abby turned back. "*Now,* Mother."

Caroline nodded and reluctantly followed Abby into the kitchen. "Why did you ask me to help you, Abby?" she hissed. "I was just getting to know Mr. Logan."

"Because he's a guest and you were about to give

him the third degree." Abby filled the water tank of the coffeemaker.

"That's not true. I was just making conversation. By the way, I saw all those packages with the Rancho Del Ciel Hotel logo." Her eyes narrowed. "Don't tell me you and Jeffrey were there?"

"Yes," Abby answered dreamily. "It's such a lovely place, I hated to come home."

"Abby, don't tell me you spent the night with Mr. Logan?"

"Yes, I did," Abby answered, turning the water tap on loud enough to drown their conversation.

"How could you? I wanted him for Kate!" her mother wailed.

"I know." Abby found herself smiling. "But it seems he wanted me."

Her mother's eyes widened. "You've changed, Abby. I hardly recognize you anymore. In fact, you haven't been yourself since you disappeared for that week almost three months ago."

"I didn't disappear, Mother. I took a much-needed vacation. And furthermore," Abby said as she measured coffee into the coffeemaker, "I don't intend to answer any more questions about what I do and whom I do it with."

Abby ignored her mother's outraged gasp, took a small container of cream out of the refrigerator and put it on a tea tray. She was about to open the cupboard for cups and saucers, when Jeff appeared in the doorway.

"Can I help?"

"Yes, you can," Abby answered. "You're just what I needed—a tall man. Whoever designs kitchen cabinets is either six feet tall or a man who doesn't understand most women are shorter than he is."

"In that case, I'm all yours," Jeff answered.

Abby's mother huffed at the interruption and sailed out of the kitchen.

"I hate to hurt my mother," Abby remarked, "but I'm tired of being treated like a child. As far as I can see, if anyone needs to grow up, it's Caroline."

Jeff came up behind her. "You're right. You aren't a child." He nuzzled the side of her neck. "Definitely all grown up."

Abby melted at the comments and turned into his arms. When he closed his arms around her, she leaned into his warmth. His solid strength and his sense of humor seemed to be the only sane things around her today. Grateful, she raised her head for his kiss. "This may be the wrong time and the wrong place," she murmured as she pulled away, "but I can't seem to care."

"It's always the right time and place for two people who care about each other." He pulled her back into his arms. "Now, be honest," he teased. "What is there about me that you like?"

"Mom." Kate's demanding voice broke the magic of the moment. She stood in the kitchen doorway. "Dad and Sebastian said they'd be through talking in a minute and that they'd like some coffee, too."

Good Lord! Taken aback at the realization that all she could think of was Jeff, Abby moved out of his arms. How could she have forgotten Richard and Sebastian, when they were in the next room?

"Of course," Abby answered, reaching for a tray. She exchanged a hurried glance with the man who now occupied her waking and sleeping hours. Barely concealing a smile, he reached for cups and saucers.

"Kate, please see if we have any more of those Girl Scout cookies in the freezer."

Abby led the way into the living room and cleared off the coffee table. "Kate, why don't you tell your father that coffee is ready. Call your grandmother, too."

"I don't know why she's so upset, but Grandma said to tell you she may never come out of her room again."

"She will when she smells the coffee," Abby answered dryly.

"Abby, sweetheart!" Richard Carson, her ex-husband, strode into the room, grabbed Abby around the waist and kissed her soundly. Behind him, Kate moved to Sebastian's side.

Abby laughed. "You don't change much, do you, Richard?" she said fondly, rumpling his brown hair that was turning white at his temples. He was the same old Richard, long hair tied back into a ponytail, and wearing the casual clothing that branded him a rebel. "But I do believe you've gained a few pounds."

"Maybe," he answered happily, "but that's what you like about me, right?" With his arm around Abby's shoulder, he turned to Jeff. "I've already met Sebastian. Why don't you introduce me to this young man?"

"Of course," Abby answered. *Young man!* Her ex-husband, her lover and her would-be suitor were all looking expectantly at her. Abby felt foolish and exposed.

"Jeff, I'd like you to meet Richard Carson, Kate's father. Richard, this is Jeffrey Logan, a friend of mine."

"Hi, nice to meet you," Richard said without taking his arm from Abby's shoulder. "Have you two known each other long?"

"Not too long—" Jeff began casually.

"We met on vacation a few months ago, and have just renewed our acquaintanceship," Abby interjected.

She gestured to Sebastian. "Jeff, you remember Sebastian Curtis, don't you?"

"Yes," he answered, shaking Sebastian's hand. "We met at the Realtor's dinner."

Abby felt a tenseness in the air when she gazed at her ex-husband. She'd been right. Something was wrong. "Coffee?" She sat down on the upholstered sofa and started to fill cups. "Help yourselves to cream and sugar. Kate's found us some cookies."

The silence that fell as they sipped hot coffee made Abby nervous. It was time to take the bull by the horns and get whatever it was out in the open.

"What brings you to Los Angeles, Richard?"

"Kate asked me to come. I decided now was as good a time as any to take a vacation, so I packed up and flew out here." He gestured to a suitcase by the entry. "I knew you wouldn't mind if I stayed with you for a few days."

"Of course not. You know you're always welcome." Abby turned her gaze on her daughter. "Kate, is there something you want to tell me?"

"I've wanted to talk to you all week, but you've been too busy to listen!"

Abby thought for a minute. Kate was only partially correct. Reluctant to hear Sebastian's marriage proposal, Abby *had* been trying to avoid him. As for Kate, even if she had tried to talk to her, Abby had been too engrossed with Jeff to think of anything but him.

Belatedly, she avoided Jeff's gaze. The other three people she cared about the most seemed to be studying her closely. Was the night she'd spent with Jeff so apparent?

Richard was eyeing her fondly. His blue eyes twinkled as if he had a secret. Whatever the secret was, from the look in his eyes, Abby sensed it affected her.

Sebastian, a man with old-world Austrian charm who had turned into a friend, returned her gaze soberly. He was a good man, and certainly worthy of consideration. But he wasn't Jeff.

Kate, her blue eyes so like her father's, was looking at Abby apprehensively.

And Jeff, whose eyes spoke volumes, was regarding her with compassion.

"Would you rather I leave?" he asked quietly. "If this is going to be a family conference, maybe you'd rather be alone." He set his empty cup on the coffee table and started to rise.

Abby reacted as if she'd been stung by a bee. Her sixth sense told her whatever was going on wasn't going to be easy to take. She needed Jeff's moral support more than ever.

"Not at all," she told him. "Please stay. I'm sure this won't take long. Now, Richard, why don't you start. What was so important that it brought you to Los Angeles so suddenly?"

Her former husband shrugged. "Maybe we should let Sebastian and Kate tell you."

Sebastian and Kate?

"Yes, of course." Sebastian took a deep breath. "Abby, what I have to tell you may come as a surprise to you, but believe me when I tell you it comes from my heart. I've given it a great deal of thought."

Abby braced herself for what was coming next—Sebastian's marriage proposal. On the other hand, surely a man like Sebastian wouldn't declare himself in front of her former husband, would he?

Embarrassed, she remembered considering marrying Sebastian. Had she led him on too long? Dazed, she dreaded the idea of his forthcoming marriage proposal and wondered how she could turn him down lightly. She glanced over at Jeff's bemused smile and mustered a smile of her own. "Please go on, Sebastian."

"I find myself in a peculiar situation, Abby. One I never would have dreamt would happen to me. That is, until I met you and your wonderful little family."

Abby bit back an urge to giggle. What would he think of her if he knew how she'd spent most of the night in Jeff's arms? "Thank you. As a matter of fact, I've thought of you as a dear friend, too."

"I'm happy to hear you say that, because I would hate to have you consider me a fool."

"I would never do that." Whatever had made Sebastian think she would consider him a fool?

"You mean you've guessed?" A broad smile came over his face. "I didn't think I was so transparent."

Abby smiled, a fond smile, but one she hoped that he couldn't possibly misinterpret. "Not all things are easy to hide. I suppose I did know you had something on your mind."

"Yes, I have." Sebastian took a deep breath. "As you know, I am a widower after twenty years of marriage. My dream was to have children, but it was not to be."

Abby made the appropriate sympathetic sounds. What did Richard have to do with this? she wondered. She glanced at her former husband, who looked as if butter could melt in his mouth.

"Not too long ago," Sebastian went on, "I realized my dreams of having a wife and children are within my grasp after all.''

Jeff quietly rose and moved to stand behind Abby's chair. Abby didn't know why. She must have missed something in the conversation. In any case, she was grateful for Jeff's solid, reassuring presence behind her.

To Abby's astonishment, Sebastian took one of Kate's hands in his. "If I don't say this now, I don't know if I'll have the courage to say it later."

Surprised at the way Kate clung to Sebastian's hand, Abby motioned him to continue. Her mind whirled with ways she could turn Sebastian down gently without causing him too much disappointment. After a night in Jeff's arms, she'd realized she wasn't ready to grow old, nor to grow old alongside Sebastian.

Sebastian's facial expression grew determined. He took a deep breath and plunged on. "I have come to ask you and Kate's father for permission to marry Kate."

Abby tried to swallow her astonishment. "Kate?"

Chapter Seven

"Any problems, Abby?"

If only Dr. Beth Gardner knew what had transpired in the three weeks since she'd last been in. But Abby replied, "Not really. Only that when things get too stressful, some foods don't seem to agree with me."

"Well, at least it's keeping your weight down," her doctor said with a sympathetic smile. She made a note on Abby's chart. "It might help if you try to stay out of stressful situations. Anything else?"

"No," Abby answered, mindful that the situation she'd managed to find herself in was going to linger for months to come. "Outside of having to watch what I eat, I feel wonderful. Actually, I feel happier now than when I had Kate."

"How is Kate these days?"

"Believe it or not, she's getting married soon. And the irony of it all is that she's marrying a man I thought was interested in me!" Abby caught her doctor's incredulous look. "Honestly—I'm not joking."

"Not to the young man who fathered your baby, I hope?"

"Goodness, no." Strangely enough, she laughed. "Kate's in love with Sebastian Curtis, a charming older man. Madly in love."

"Nothing surprises me anymore," Beth answered. "Now that it's spring, I guess love is in the air. How about you? Still in love with the father of your baby?"

"I don't know if you can call it love," Abby answered with a rueful smile. "More the idea of love. Not that I think it's the right thing at this stage in my life."

"And you still don't want the father to know?"

"I'm not sure," Abby answered. "At first, I thought Jeff was too much like my first husband—stuck in daydreams and thinking only of himself. I decided I was better off raising this child alone than worrying about when and if Jeff would change his mind and move on to something else. Now, I've begun to see another side of him."

She thought about the years Jeff had given to his father's dream of having Jeff take over when it was time for him to retire. And Jeff's reluctance to just walk away and pursue his own dreams. Certainly, she had to give him credit for that. "You know, strangely enough, although Jeff's also a dreamer, he seems more responsible than Richard ever was."

Beth put aside Abby's chart. "It's none of my business, Abby, but since we're friends as well as doctor and patient, I feel I can speak to you freely. Right?''

Abby's heart sank. "Is something wrong with the baby?"

"Not at all. If there were, I'd tell you. In fact, you're one of the luckier older mothers."

One of the luckier older mothers. Abby thought about that for a moment. Maybe she shouldn't be so happy about having a baby at her age, but she was. It was a second chance to be the kind of mother she would have liked to have been when she was carrying Kate. Time to be with her child instead of working during the day and going to school at night. Time to teach and to play. Given that she was on her own too often, it was a blessing Kate had turned out to be so mature and well adjusted.

"I just wanted to suggest that it's time you let the baby's father in on the secret, Abby. That is, if you care about this man as much as I think you do. You'll be a healthier and happier mother with someone around who cares for you, instead of trying to go it alone." Beth leaned toward Abby and touched her hand. "He does care for you, doesn't he?"

ABBY COULDN'T IGNORE the problems of love. She paused in front of the medical building, shielded her eyes from the afternoon glare and thought about her doctor's question.

She'd never doubted Jeff cared for her in his own way. But was she only a woman he'd chosen to romance before he moved on to someone else? The longer she thought about it, the more she realized he'd never actually said he loved her. But then, she hadn't told him she loved him, either.

Was she in love with him? she wondered, or just with the miracle of finding passion at her age?

Yesterday, she had been on the verge of telling him how much she cared for him—until she'd noticed the cold expression that came over his face when Richard called him a "young man." She'd sensed a wariness between them, maybe even a hint of jealousy. Another kind of stress she didn't need.

It wasn't a matter of making choices between past and current lovers, she thought as she started down the street. In spite of their divorce, Richard had remained someone special in her life. He was as comfortable as an old shoe, an unreliable but loved older brother. She couldn't give him up completely, not even for Jeff.

Two doors down from the medical building, a baby store beckoned her. She remembered the thrift shop furniture she'd bought for Kate, the serviceable baby clothing, and the small dime-store dolls Kate had pretended were her sisters. How different they had all been from the display in this window!

The bright maple crib was decorated in a frothy white-and-green dimity with yellow and green ribbons threaded through the lace flounce. The changing table echoed the colors of the crib; the lamps alongside it were colorful red, green and yellow balloons. This time, and with this child, she vowed, there would be pleasure instead of sadness, laughter instead of tears.

She opened the door and walked into the magical kingdom.

A rocking chair occupied a corner where a king-size teddy bear shared the place of honor with Raggedy Andy. A small bookcase held small children's picture books. All fine for a little girl, Abby thought with a smile, but what if her baby was a boy? A tiny boy with golden-brown hair, who resembled his father? Maybe Beth was right. It was time to tell Jeff about the baby.

But how? And when?

JEFF WAS PASSING by a storefront window when he caught a glimpse of a woman inside, a woman who looked an awful lot like Abby. He glanced up to the store name. A baby shop? What was Abby doing there?

Kate.

Maybe Kate is pregnant, he thought, wincing as he opened the door. One more problem for Abby to deal with—not that she needed another. Or maybe she was buying a shower gift for someone. He brightened at the thought.

"Hi, Abby! Shopping?"

Shaken out of her reverie, Abby blinked. Of all the people she hadn't expected to see, Jeff headed the list. She'd already mentally agreed with her doctor; she intended to tell him about the baby. She just wasn't ready, nor had she planned on the shop being the place for the announcement.

Concerned at her preoccupation, Jeff eyed her with concern. "Are you okay? There was something different about you all weekend."

She tried to recall the weekend. Except for Sebastian's bombshell, she was sure she'd taken everything in her stride. "I'm fine. What makes you think something is wrong?"

"Well, you were kind of preoccupied and teary."

"Just like a man," Abby answered with a wry, relieved smile. "I wasn't crying. I was trying hard not to laugh with relief when I realized Sebastian wasn't going to propose to me. I had been trying to figure out how to let him down gently. Thank goodness I didn't have to."

"You don't say?" Jeff eyed her doubtfully. "You still seem preoccupied. Something on your mind? Anything I can do to help?"

"Yes, you can," Abby answered, glancing around her. Maybe a baby shop *was* the right place. The way her stomach was reacting to unexpectedly seeing Jeff, it was time to let go of a stressful secret. Maybe the time had come to tell him her secret.

"Buying a gift for someone?"

Abby nodded.

"Not Kate, I hope?"

While she paused to consider how to tell Jeff about the baby, she watched him glance around the shop. "I never knew kids needed so many things."

"That's because you've never been around a

baby," Abby answered, following his gaze around the well-stocked shop. There was everything a baby could possibly need, from christening clothes to diapers. There was infant furniture from cribs to lamps and everything in between. In one corner, for shoppers, two padded adult rattan rocking chairs were positioned beside a matching table.

"How did you know I was in here?"

"I'd just come out of my dentist's building down the street and I saw you come in here."

Jeff wandered over to a toy train display and picked up the engine. "I used to have one of these when I was a kid. But mine was metal—this one's made of wood."

"That's because wood is safer. Small children won't hurt themselves."

"Sounds reasonable." He put back the toy engine and picked up a stuffed bear to study its expression. "This one resembles someone I know," he said, glancing at Abby with a teasing smile. "He looks pretty thoughtful, too."

Now was a good time to give him the news, Abby decided as a familiar nursery song played in the background. "Maybe we should find someplace quiet to talk," Abby said. "I have something to tell you."

"Sure," Jeff answered agreeably. "I wouldn't mind having you to myself for a while. How about right over there?" He gestured to the rocking chairs. "So, who's the lucky baby you're shopping for?"

Before Abby could answer, the store clerk hurried

over to them with a small tray in her hands. "Oh, there you are, Mrs. Carson! I brought you a cup of tea and a few dry crackers to help settle your stomach. I'm sure you're going to feel better in a few minutes. And, oh, yes, the custom-made baby furniture you ordered will be ready for you long before your baby is due."

She beamed at Abby, then turned her attention to Jeff. "We have a few new fathers who seem to suffer from morning sickness—just like their wives," she said with a sympathetic smile. "Is this your first?"

"My first?" Shocked at the question, Jeff froze and felt the blood drain from his face. "My first what?"

"Oh, dear," the clerk fluttered. "I didn't mean to upset you. Would you like me to bring you a cup of tea and some crackers, too?"

"Er...no, thanks," Jeff managed to say as soon as his heart slowed down. Abby needed tea and crackers to settle her stomach! She'd ordered baby furniture for a baby *she* was expecting? And the sales clerk thought *he* was the baby's father?

Cold fingers played a staccato up and down his spine as he considered Abby. He'd suspected there was something going on with her, but never in his wildest dreams had he imagined something like this. He swallowed hard and waited until the store clerk apologized again and disappeared behind a curtain.

"*Are* you expecting a baby, Abby?" He gazed at her trim figure in disbelief. If she was pregnant, she hadn't shown it the night he'd "kidnapped" her. Nor did she show it now. Of course, she *was* wearing a loose coat....

Abby's stomach roiled. She took a sip of tea to quiet the internal waves of protest. "Yes, I am."

"I hate to ask such a personal question," he said cautiously, "but how far along are you?"

"About two months, give or take a week," she answered, swallowing the lump in her throat.

Jeff bounded out of the rocking chair so forcefully that the chair bounced back against the wall. The little stuffed teddy bear whose nose he'd been petting dropped out of his hands, and Raggedy Andy flew into the air. Mesmerized, he stood gazing at Abby's middle. His thoughts awhirl, he wasn't sure how he felt about her answer. After all, he thought, adding up the weeks in his head, two months would make him the father!

"Are you sure?" he whispered after a quick look around to see if anyone was listening. "I may sound like a heel, Abby, but I have to tell you, this is the last thing I expected to hear."

"I'm sure. Actually, I was just as surprised to find out I'm pregnant as you are." Abby set the cup on the table and twisted a Winnie-the-Pooh paper napkin between her fingers. "I've taken several tests, and they all came out positive."

He rubbed his forehead. "But how could this have happened? I used protection in Acapulco. I know I did."

"These things can happen, anyway," Abby replied with a rueful half smile. "When we were at the Rancho Del Ciel, do you remember asking me if I needed protection?"

Jeff cringed at the intimate question. His gaze darted to the flimsy curtain that separated the shop from the back room. Even the stuffed animals in the background seemed to be listening for his answer. "What does that have to do with...?" Words failed him.

"And do you remember my answer?"

"Vaguely," he answered, trying hard to recall their conversation. It was no use. All he *could* remember was taking off Abby's T-shirt. The rest of the scene blended into passionate kisses and heated, tangled limbs. "I'm afraid I wasn't thinking too clearly at the time. I had something else on my mind."

"I know, so did I," she agreed. "But the reason I said 'no' was because I knew it was already too late." She gently touched her abdomen.

Jeff blinked. "Why didn't you tell me then?"

"At first I wasn't sure about the baby, and after I found out, I didn't know how to tell you," Abby answered simply. "I'm sorry if I've upset you."

Upset him! That was the understatement of the year, Jeff thought, his eyes glued to Abby's middle.

"And after we met again at the banquet? Did you know then?"

She shook her head. "I didn't know if I should tell you, or, frankly, if you wanted to know. We only knew each other under assumed names. Under the circumstances, I felt we were practically strangers.''

Jeff's mind whirled at the prospect of fatherhood. "Of course I would want to know. At least, I think I would...I do. What kind of a man do you think I am?"

"I'm sorry," Abby replied. "Maybe I should have told you sooner, but I just made up my mind today to tell you. It became a matter of the right time and place." She gazed around the baby shop. "I just didn't dream it would be here, or that a sales-clerk would do the honors."

Jeff glanced warily at Abby's middle again. A child of his rested there, his first. And heaven help him, he didn't know what to think about the revelation.

He hadn't expected to become a father, and certainly not before he was ready to get married and settle down. His own family experience hadn't been one he was in a hurry to duplicate. He hadn't been anxious to follow the example set by his feuding parents, either.

But a child of his own! The idea rattled him. Not that he had anything against children, but they just hadn't figured into his plans. Besides, if he eventually decided to follow his father into the Logan hotel business, he'd never be in one place long enough to enjoy any children anyway. Just like his own father had been with him.

He gazed long and hard around the shop, then at Abby. No matter how he felt about fatherhood, at least there was no doubt in his mind he was about to become a father.

"Are you happy about the baby, Abby?" he asked, his eyes searching hers.

"Yes, I am," Abby answered. "I don't want you to think I regret a minute of what happened between us—including the baby. He's given me a new lease on life—just when I thought the happier times in my life were behind me."

"He? You mean it's a boy?"

"No, it was just a figure of speech. Would you mind if she turned out to be a girl?"

Jeff shook his head. He glanced at the wooden toy train and the row of soft, cloth dolls on a shelf behind it. At the stacks of infant diapers and tiny garments and items he couldn't even identify. Enough baby stuff to make a man's head spin. Abby was right, maybe the problem was that he'd never been around babies. Heaven help the kid.

The pieces of the puzzle that was Abby began to fall into place for him as he looked at her.

For a few minutes back at the cottage—now that he thought about it—he had noticed for a minute that there had been a new fullness to Abby's breasts when he was making love to her. It was a thought he'd dismissed when he couldn't actually recall how she'd looked under moonlit skies.

There were her remarks at dinner that night about watching her weight when she already had a figure that fulfilled any man's dreams, including his. Even the waiter had looked surprised.

Then there were Abby's mood swings. She'd told him she'd been laughing at herself when Sebastian had surprised them all by asking for Kate's hand in marriage. Strangely enough, by that time he'd been so in tune with Abby's moods that he'd sensed there had been tears behind her laughter. Did pregnancy do that to a woman?

It wasn't only himself he was concerned about now, he realized. There was Abby and now a child of his to consider.

As she watched changing emotions grip Jeff, Abby's heart was troubled. His surprised reaction wasn't totally unexpected, but she'd hoped for something more than his silence. It showed her that he wasn't pleased at the idea of impending fatherhood. She put her half-empty tea cup aside and started to rise.

"Where are you going, Abby? We need to talk about this."

"Not now," she answered, when two shoppers entered the store. "And not when you have mixed feelings about the baby. But let me tell you this," she added firmly, "I did okay raising Kate by myself, and I'll be fine with this baby, too. You don't have to worry about us."

Before Jeff could answer, she made her way out of the store.

Jeff knew by Abby's abrupt departure that he was in trouble—not that he blamed Abby. Taken by surprise, he'd behaved like a first-class jerk. Instead of telling Abby how pleased he was to hear about the baby, he'd let her down. He'd let her think he wasn't pleased at the idea of fatherhood. Even though he hadn't expected to become a father at this stage in his life, he *was* pleased. It was just that he needed some time to come to grips with Abby's announcement and his future role in Abby's life.

He gazed around him at some of the familiar toys of his own childhood. Throughout his younger years, he'd often thought that when he had children of his own he'd be a better father to them than his own father was to him. That he'd take time to show that he loved and cared about his children, that he would listen to them, support their decisions. And now that he had the chance, he'd blown it!

Abby. He came to with a start. He'd let her leave without telling her how he felt about the baby. He had to catch up with her...now.

"Oh, Mr. Carson, wait a minute. I expected to see Mrs. Carson, but you'll do. I have your wife's receipt for the baby's crib." The shop clerk rushed over to Jeff and beamed at him, before she turned away to wait on the other customers. "I hope we'll see more of you in the future. It's so nice to see an involved father."

Jeff shook his head and rushed out the door. It was a good thing *someone* thought he was an involved father. Now he had to make Abby believe that he wanted to be one.

He caught up with her at the corner. "Abby, we have to talk."

Abby shook her head and tried to pull away. "We

can talk about this some other time, if you insist. Right now, I have to get back to the office.''

''Not before you talk to me.''

Abby hesitated. ''About what?''

Now that Jeff appeared to be in a state of shock, what was there to talk about? She watched him take a deep breath, closed her eyes and again started to turn away.

''Abby, you have to take the time to at least listen to me for a minute,'' he said, grabbing her arm. ''Please!''

Abby paused. ''Why?''

''Because I want to ask you to marry me.''

Chapter Eight

Abby hesitated. She'd done what her conscience had told her she should do. But marry him for the baby's sake? That was another story. One failed marriage was enough. "I'm sorry, I can't marry you."

Jeff exploded. "Why not, for pity's sake?" If Abby had cut him off at the knees, he couldn't have felt worse than he did now.

"Among other things, I'm not sure you're ready to be a father," she answered quietly. "If that bothers you, I'm sorry."

"I'm telling you I want to be a husband and a father, and you're still turning me down?"

She regarded him silently.

"I'm not going to let you go until you listen to me, Abby. There's too much at stake here. All you need to do is say 'yes,' and I'll show you just what kind of a husband and father I can be. Come with me." He took her hand and started off down the street.

"Where are we going?"

"Somewhere where we can talk. If I can't convince you to marry me now, you're still going to have to let me help you."

Abby held back. "Help me with what, for heaven's sake? I can handle it. After all, this isn't going to be my first child."

"Maybe not," he answered, squaring his jaw. "But this is my first. I intend to see to it that you take care of yourself properly. Tea and soda crackers won't cut it."

Abby's mind went into a tailspin. Visions of Jeff dogging her footsteps, visiting her doctor with her, and making certain she ate and slept properly were more than she could handle. "No, you're not!"

"Yes. I am," he answered firmly. "And furthermore, I'm going to show you just how involved a husband and a father I can be. And when I get through, I'm damn sure you'll reconsider. So, if I can show you I can be the kind of father you want me to be, will it change your mind?"

"It depends," she said cautiously. "I hope you're not planning on doing anything foolish."

"You'll see. And one more thing. I'm through calling the baby 'it.' If it's all right with you, I'd like to call him Patrick."

Bemused, Abby nodded.

"Now, if you want to go somewhere more private, we can walk over to the Logan Wilshire and discuss this in my suite. I was on my way over there anyway when I saw you through the shop window."

He thought of the owner's suite at the hotel. And the exciting and wonderful ways he had hoped to spend the evening there with Abby. Before the sky had fallen in on him.

He gazed into Abby's skeptical green eyes. She might not be convinced, but it looked as if she was wavering just a little. Good. One way or another, he had the feeling that he was about to get the chance to convince her he was serious.

He gave it his last and best shot. "This isn't only about a romance, Abby," he added. "It's about a family—ours. So, what do you say? Do we have a deal?"

Abby didn't know what to say. She told him about the baby because she understood that the baby was just as much his child as hers. And now that he'd given the baby a name, the ties that bound the three of them seemed more real than ever.

Maybe she did owe him more. Even if she eventually decided not to marry him, she still owed him a chance to show her that he could be a good father. As for Jeff making a loving husband... She blushed at the memory of his hands sliding around her waist, his body coming over hers and making her his. Of passionate kisses, bare skin sliding over bare skin. Of whispered words of endearment.

Oh yes, Jeff had already convinced her he would make a wonderful husband. But first things first. He had to show her he could make a good father.

"Before you say anything, Abby," he said before she could answer, "I'd just like to make one more important point. You obviously care for me a great deal or you wouldn't have let me make love to you at the cottage. No, don't deny it," he said, when she blushed and started to tell him that she had to draw the line between desire and commitment. "You know I'm right. As for the night we first met, and the wonderful hours we spent together, we can blame it on the new moon if you want to."

He took her unresisting hands in his, drew her close and tenderly brushed the back of his hand across her rose-petal soft cheek. "I do care for you, Abby," he murmured as he bent to kiss her throat. "Believe it."

Afraid to raise false hopes, Abby's gaze locked with his. She was tempted to walk away, to stay away until after the baby was born. If only her senses weren't crying out to have his strong arms around her, holding her while they made love. Crying out for the taste of his lips on hers, for his male scent, for the sound of his voice whispering soft words of affection into her ear.

She gazed into his clear brandy-colored eyes. The depth of the desire she saw there struck a responsive chord in her. The tender loving she'd longed for was within her reach. Whatever had gone before became a beginning. The moment now became everything. Drawn to his strong male appeal, every ounce of her pragmatic reservations vanished. As if she were a novice in the game of love and he the leader, she heard herself saying, "Okay, I'll give you thirty days."

His eyes lit up with a warmth that moved her heart. "Great."

Thirty days, Abby mused. Her pulse quickened. A month. It was such a small part of a lifetime. Surely she owed them that much.

The sound of pedestrian and automobile traffic kept Jeff from pursuing their conversation on the way over to the hotel. Instead, he mentally rehearsed what he intended to say to Abby when they reached the suite.

When they finally reached his penthouse, the red message light on the telephone was blinking. He was tempted to ignore it, but he was in charge of the hotel, after all.

"Hold on a minute, Abby." He punched the "play" button.

His sister's voice filled the room. "Jeff, this is Elaine. I thought I'd better warn you, Dad is frosted. He says you have to come up to San Francisco and make up your mind about joining him. And this time, he said, he's not going to take 'maybe' for an answer. Call me at home later tonight if you want to talk."

He muttered his frustration and punched the "rewind" button. "I'm sorry you had to hear that, Abby. It's just Dad letting off steam again."

"Your sister sounded pretty serious. Maybe you ought to call your father now."

"There's no hurry," Jeff replied, scowling at the telephone. "He wants me to join him on his annual tour of the Logan properties. I've been putting him off. I feel like hell about it, but I'm not going to commit myself to following in his footsteps. Not yet, anyhow. And not until I'm sure that's what I want to do for the rest of my life.''

He gazed helplessly around a room that was the height of luxury but devoid of personal touches. ''Suites like this are only places to sleep in—nothing more. The idea of spending my working days like this is more than I can handle.

''I know I may sound ungrateful,'' he added, ''but until you showed me the furnished cottage in Westwood, I'd never found a place I could call home. A place where I could put down roots.''

Abby gazed around her. ''The suite is lovely, but you're right. It certainly doesn't look anything like you.''

''How *do* I look, Abby?'' he asked, wondering what she saw in him. And why what she saw wasn't enough to convince her that he'd be a credible and involved father and husband.

She tilted her head and studied him as if it were the first time they'd met. ''I think you're intelligent, warm and witty. But you're also a man who hasn't been able to decide on who he really is or what he wants out of life. As for this suite—'' she gestured around her ''—if home is where your heart is, I agree with you. This obviously isn't the place.''

''You're right,'' he added bitterly. ''Sometimes I have to stop to remember just what hotel and which city I'm in.''

Jeff returned her solemn gaze. For a minute, he'd thought she was going to reconsider turning him down. It had to be more than his stupid proposal of marriage that turned her off. But what was a guy to do when the news he was going to be a father came out of left field?

"You're not worried about what your family or your ex will think about us, are you?"

"Of course not. Richard has nothing to do with this. We're friends. He has his life and I have mine."

"You may not realize it, Abby, but Richard still cares for you."

"I know he does," she answered. Jeff was a male defending his territory, but how could she tell him that there was no territory for him to defend? "And I care for him, but not in the way you're suggesting. I told you before, we're very good friends."

"I overheard the two of you talking the other day about the time you were married to each other. He may have thought your life together was a hoot, but it didn't look to me as if you enjoyed recalling the marriage."

"Not particularly," she answered. "But I don't understand what that has to do with us."

He took her cold hands in his and gently warmed them between his own. "One good thing I've learned from my father is never to play a game that I didn't hope to win. And this is one game I intend to win. So, I want you to know, no matter what your life was like with Richard, I'm not Richard. If you give me a chance, I'll prove it to you. As far as money goes, it's no problem. And as for the baby, I'm sure I can learn to be a damn good father. Best of all," he said with a wry smile, "you can grow old with me instead of Sebastian."

Abby shook her head. "Those aren't the only reasons I can't marry you. It wasn't the lack of money that came between Richard and myself. We both agreed that we had no future together. And I'm not foolish enough to try to recapture my youth. What is a problem is that you and I have different natures. I'll admit I'm a worrier and a planner, but you seem to take life one day at a time. I can't live that way again."

Jeff listened, but nothing Abby said deterred him. At least, not yet. He'd had enough talking.

"Okay, Abby, we'll do it your way. If you agree to keep an open mind for thirty days, I'm going to show you we belong together."

"Only for thirty days," she repeated as she fought for sanity. An impossible state considering what Jeff's hands and lips were doing to her.

"I wouldn't take bets on that time frame, if I were you," he murmured. "I warn you, I'm shooting for something more permanent." He picked her up in his arms and headed for the huge damask-covered king-size bed that she'd glimpsed in an adjacent room.

Somewhere between the living room and the bedroom, Abby lost the rest of her clothing—and her reasons why she and Jeff didn't belong together.

"So, where did we leave off?" Jeff murmured. He unbuttoned his shirt and impatiently pulled it off his shoulders. He removed the rest of his clothing and joined her on the bed. When she reached for him, he bent over and peered at her. "I seem to remember it was right about…here." He fingered the sensitive spot on her neck.

Abby shivered with desire when Jeff's lips kissed her nape. "Or maybe it was right about…here." He moved on to taste the corner of her eyes. When she shivered again, he tilted her head and kissed the curve of her neck.

Abby felt as if she were living a dream—a dream from which she didn't ever want to awaken. She was filled with a mindless longing to make love with him again, to take him to her, to feel his slick skin create sexual electricity as he slid across her bare skin and made her his. With a sigh, she drew him even closer, until there wasn't room for a whisper of air between them. "No, I think it was right about here." She motioned to her breasts.

Jeff leaned back on his elbow, gazed at her in mock concentration. "Are you sure? I wouldn't want to miss a spot."

"I'm very sure," she answered, holding out her arms to pull him back over her.

His expression suddenly serious, Jeff seemed to hesitate. "I wouldn't want to do anything to hurt you or Patrick."

"You can't hurt us by loving me," Abby answered. "But if you're not sure, then let me convince you."

With a laugh, he lay back on the bed and pulled

her over him. He gazed fondly into her eyes. "Do your worst, sweetheart. I'm all yours."

Abby smiled. "I will." She cupped his face between her hands and kissed him with all the pent-up longing inside her. What difference did it make if he wasn't her idea of the ideal father and husband? Hadn't he promised to show her that he could be? As far as that went, she thought fleetingly, she could hardly have been his idea of perfection, either.

But, for better or worse, a horoscope had brought them together. Or was it chance? She didn't care. This was her fantasy come to life. For now, that knowledge was enough to keep her in his arms.

She slowly tongued his skin from his brow down to his chin, exacting sweet revenge in tiny bites when he stirred restlessly under her.

"Had enough?" she whispered.

"No, ma'am," he answered with a shaky laugh. "Not yet, and maybe not ever."

With a wicked smile, Abby renewed her efforts. She went on to explore his chest with her fingers and her tongue, reveling in the salty taste of him. Reluctant to let the moment and the sensations stirring through her go, she massaged his waist, his hips, until he groaned with desire. "Had enough yet?" she said into the sexual tension that had built up between them.

"Not nearly enough," he gasped, "but I think I've gotten the message." He put his hands around her waist and turned her onto her back.

"Now, Abby?" His warm, tender hands moved over her until her every nerve ending cried for relief.

"Now," she whispered with a sigh of contentment.

The sound seemed to drive him over the edge. He slowly moved over her and joined them in a dance as old as yesterday, as new as tomorrow. Her own desire reached a crescendo of sensation. Moments later, she felt as if she had shattered into a thousand pieces.

"So tell me," Jeff said, when, for the moment, desire ebbed and she lay cradled in his arms. "Are you convinced?"

"Convinced of what?" Abby asked when her nerve endings had stopped tingling. He was a wonderful lover, but that wasn't what the thirty days were supposed to be about.

He was watching her, obviously expecting her to answer "yes." Something wicked inside her wanted to prolong the moment. "Maybe we should try again."

"It was good enough to convince me," he grinned knowingly. "But if you think you need any more convincing, give me a few minutes."

Abby sighed and idly twisted her fingers in the strand of golden-brown hair that hung over his forehead. The look in his eyes suggested that he didn't need a few minutes to take her in his arms again. "On the other hand, I think you've already convinced me, about this part at least. The part about fatherhood is another story."

"This first part was only to bind our agreement. And this," he added, "is to give you something to remember me by."

He blew gently on the rosy hollow between her breasts, then tongued his way down to her waist. "As for the rest of the afternoon, I have a few other plans for us."

"I'm starved," Abby protested feebly. "And I have an appointment to see a client this evening."

"No fair, Abby," he teased. "If you want to be a success, you have to concentrate on one subject at a time. Right now, the subject at hand is you and me."

"I wish," she answered. She loved every moment of their bedroom play, but there was more to their encounter than a test of sexual compatibility. She'd never had any doubts on that subject. It was tomorrow, and his role as a father, that still troubled her. "As a matter of fact, I'm afraid I won't be able to spend a lot of time with you this week. There are still some loose ends to tie up for Kate's wedding."

"Isn't your ex staying until the wedding?" He left off his exploration of her body.

"Of course. Richard would never leave before Kate's wedding." Good heavens, she thought gazing into Jeff's darkened eyes. How could he be so concerned over Richard's presence when she'd just shown him how much she cared for *him?* "Why do you want to know?"

"Can't he help out and leave you some free time? Or are you planning on doing everything yourself?"

Abby sobered at the tight sound in Jeff's voice that she heard whenever he mentioned her ex-husband. "You can't possibly be jealous of Richard! I've told you, he and I are the best of friends, but that's all."

"Have you told him about us?" he asked, casually running his fingers over her throat.

"No, but I'm sure he's guessed by now." Abby stared at him. This was becoming more serious than she'd thought.

"And Patrick?"

"Not about the baby, either. But I suppose he's bound to find out sooner or later."

Suddenly, Abby was disturbed at the idea that Richard might not be as happy about the baby as she was.

Jeff couldn't hide his frustration. He suspected, as only one man reading another could suspect, that given a chance, Abby's ex-husband would try to win her back. The last thing Jeff wanted was to have Richard Carson trade on the romance that surrounded a wedding to try to persuade Abby to marry him again. "Abby, let's get married right away. Then it won't make any difference who finds out about us."

"It won't make a difference who knows, anyway. Not to me," she answered. "It's a little late for either of us to worry what people might say. And if it's Richard you're talking about, you can forget it. We've always wanted the best for each other. I told you, he's a dear friend."

"I want the best for you too, Abby. If you'd only let me show you how much. Not only today, but every day for the rest of our lives." Resigned to her silence, Jeff sighed when she didn't reply. "I wish you'd take some time for yourself, ease up a little."

"After Kate's wedding, I promise. After that, I intend to take some time off for R and R."

What more could she tell him to make him understand the way she and her ex-husband felt about each other? Abby wondered. Richard was her past. And no matter how much she might doubt that Jeff was ready to be a father, he *was* part of her future.

"Glad to hear it," Jeff answered. "As long as you include me in your rest and relaxation, I'll go along with you. As a matter of fact, I'll be busy for a while, too. I have a few more plans of my own to make. But there's going to be lots of time for us, if I have anything to say about it. And for the care and feeding of Patrick, too."

"Remember, we agreed to thirty days."

"Who knows," Jeff answered with a glint in his eyes. "Maybe it will turn out to be for a lifetime."

Abby tested the word *lifetime,* surprised there were no warning bells ringing.

She gazed into his eyes—eyes so clear, so honest, so determined to show her that he cared enough for her that he was willing to change his life. For the first time in many years, she was beginning to feel as though she could trust herself to someone else. That she had someone who wanted to watch over her.

Maybe being a father didn't come naturally to every man. With Kate, she remembered with a wistful sigh, Richard had thought bringing up a baby would be a lark. When he discovered that it wasn't, he hadn't always been willing to share the burden. Richard was certainly lovable, she'd give him that. But at this stage, Jeff seemed to be more mature than the older Richard.

"You know, it occurs to me that you don't know what you might be getting into," she said. "You've never been around small children, have you?"

"No," he answered with a grin, "but I'm a fast learner. I'll just have to get some hands-on experience."

Abby smiled. "I don't think you're going to last long. Men seldom do."

"You don't know me very well, sweetheart," he said with a kiss that sent shivers up her spine. "When I make up my mind to do something, I never give up until I have the problem licked."

Abby had to grin. She knew that much about Jeff from firsthand experience. "You actually intend to start tomorrow?"

"Tomorrow," Jeff agreed. He eyed Abby. She looked pleased with herself. If he didn't know what a sweet nature she had, he would have thought she actually doubted his seriousness about learning about the care and feeding of small children. If she thought he was kidding, she had another think coming. He'd never been more serious in his life.

Her mind turned back to another promise he'd

made. "I think I'll cancel my appointment." She glanced at the digital clock beside the bed, then at Jeff. "I think the few minutes you asked for are over, don't you?"

"YOU KNOW, I ACTUALLY feel hungry." Abby looked surprised as she touched her middle. "I think I could eat my way through a ten-course meal."

"Are you sure you wouldn't rather have something light?"

"That was before," she answered with a laugh. "Tonight, it's going to be the whole menu, or at least something I haven't enjoyed for a while." She had to keep herself from purring out loud. "Actually, I'm surprised at how good I feel."

"I'm glad," Jeff said, laying a warm hand over her tummy.

Abby laughed and pushed him away. "The party's over, at least for now. How about calling room service for dinner, while I shower?"

"Got it," he said reluctantly. He slid out of bed and reached for the telephone. "What would you like me to order?"

"Surprise me," she answered as she found herself admiring his tall, lithe body, and the play of muscles covered with a fine sheen from their lovemaking.

"Want to shower first?" she inquired, forgetting everything but the thought of being held in his arms. "Together?"

"Later," he answered over his shoulder. "I'll order first. Then we can pass the time until dinner arrives any way you want to. Speak now. What would you like me to order?''

''Something sinful,'' she answered absently. Gazing at Jeff's nude body, food was the last thing on her mind. Visions took over of warm water cascading over heated bodies.

''Maybe you ought not to push your luck by eating anything rich,'' Jeff said, ''or overdoing it. No use jumping into deep waters before you're sure you can swim.''

''Okay.'' Abby sighed as her hopes for a dual shower faded. ''You can join me in the shower when you're ready.''

Jeff swallowed. He was already ready, but if he joined Abby, there'd be no dinner for either of them tonight. ''I'll pass for now. Unless you need help washing your back?''

''Maybe not if I want to get fed tonight,'' she laughed. ''I really am starved. Please tell room service to hurry it up.''

Jeff contemplated her familiar pink-tinged body. ''I think I'll go down and talk to the chef myself,'' he said as he threw on a pair of jeans and a denim shirt. ''I'll be back soon.''

WHEN ABBY CAME into the living room wearing Jeff's oversize shirt and brushing her hair, she found him closing the door to the suite behind him. ''That didn't take you long,'' she said happily. ''What are we having for dinner?''

"Considering how good you were feeling, I talked it over with Franco. We decided not to tempt you with anything that might upset your stomach. We finally decided on spinach salad, and fettuccine with a light seafood sauce."

Abby's hand stopped in mid-stroke. "You didn't tell him I'm pregnant, did you?"

"Well, yes. I didn't think you'd mind. I wanted to make sure you're eating properly. Franco's wife just had a baby, and he assured me there's nothing in what I ordered that would upset you. You don't mind, do you?"

Abby grimaced. She hoped she'd never meet this Franco—she wouldn't be able to look him in the eye. "And for dessert?" she asked hopefully. Pretty soon Franco wouldn't be the only one able to tell she was pregnant.

"Sorbet."

"That's not exactly sinful, either." Abby looked at him reproachfully. "I was looking forward to something more like chocolate cake with ice cream."

"I'M STARVED."

Jeff came awake at the sound of Abby's voice. He glanced at the luminous clock beside the bed. "How can you be hungry? You ate all the dinner Franco sent up. It's three-thirty in the morning. The kitchen is empty except for a skeleton staff."

"Would it make a difference if I told you Patrick's hungry, too?" she pleaded.

Jeff peered at the complacent smile on Abby's face. "That's not fair," he said. "You can't use the baby as an excuse to get what you want—not at this time of the morning."

"Why not? You used him as an excuse to get what *you* want, or have you forgotten our agreement?"

The "gotcha" look in Abby's smile had him hooked.

"Okay," he said. "If it'll make you happy, why don't you get dressed and we'll go down to the kitchen. And on the way, I'll give you a tour of the hotel."

Abby slid out of bed. "I wish I had some more practical clothes around," she muttered. "It doesn't seem natural to take a tour at this time of the morning, dressed in a business suit or one of your shirts."

"No problem. There won't be many people around who would care what we look like," Jeff answered. "Put on the suit skirt, and I'll loan you a fresh shirt and a pair of knit slippers. Hurry up. I want to show you some of my favorite places."

"Favorite places? I thought you didn't like the hotel business."

"It's the business end I don't care for. It's the people who work in hotels that I like," he answered as he shrugged into a sweatshirt. "There are other things I like, too. You'll see."

He hurried her to the elevator. To Abby's surprise, he punched the "up" button. Before she knew it, they were on the roof of the hotel.

"Look over there." He gestured to the horizon. "What do you think of that view?"

Abby looked.

Stars twinkled against black-as-velvet skies. Overhead, resembling an oversize diamond, the new moon shone down on them in all its brilliance. Below the horizon, city lights kept watch over a sleeping city. From fifteen stories high, she felt as if they were the only two people in the world.

Jeff put his arm around Abby's shoulders and drew her close to him. "How about it?" he asked. "Have you ever seen anything so beautiful?"

"Only once before," she answered. "The night we met in Acapulco."

Chapter Nine

A glob of oatmeal sailed toward his head when he opened the door to the day care center. Instinctively, Jeff ducked. Instead of landing on his head, as someone obviously intended, the hot breakfast cereal laden with milk wound up on his shoulder. Seconds later, it slid down over the red embroidered Logan Hotel insignia on his jacket and down his gray pants to his shoe. He gazed down at the trail of oatmeal and wondered how a single tablespoon could create such a mess!

When he'd decided to get the experience needed to convince Abby that he was serious about fatherhood, he'd expected to have some fun along the way. But never, in his wildest imagination, had he counted on anything like this.

It was a sure sign that *fun* wasn't going to be the operative word around here.

Expecting another barrage of oatmeal, he cautiously made his way through the doorway to find himself standing at the entrance to a large, sunny room, peopled by what seemed to be dozens of small moving bodies. To his relief, a quick count stopped somewhere in the vicinity of twenty.

Breakfast was being served at a number of small tables and matching chairs located in the far corner of the room. Against one wall, rows of bookcases were filled with children's picture books. An enormous rug was positioned in front of the bookcases. Through an open door, he could see several infant cribs. Another door led to a small, compact kitchen. A number of small folding cots occupied another corner, along with a pile of junior-size blankets.

A quick review of the room revealed walls bright with colorful posters of cartoon characters. Green plants and vases of flowers, safely out of the reach of little hands, added green accents. The room looked cheerful enough, Jeff thought as he took it all in, but the children didn't.

At the moment, the large room looked more like a zoo with the resident pets on the loose. Two small boys were arguing over a toy Star Wars figure; one little guy was declaring his ownership and pushing another kid off a chair. At least six of the remaining children were chasing each other in a game of tag—to a chorus of eager onlookers. As for the smallest inmates in the adjoining room, from the way they were carrying on, they didn't sound any happier than their older classmates.

Two assistants, with determined smiles on their faces, were trying to shepherd the last of the children to the tables for a breakfast of orange juice and hot oatmeal.

The kid who had apparently sent his breakfast flying in Jeff's direction glowered at him.

A harried woman rushed towards Jeff. "May I help you?"

"Actually, I came here to help *you*," Jeff said with a hopeful smile. "As a volunteer," he hurried to add, when she looked bewildered and started to speak.

"Volunteer? My goodness, this is the first time..." Her voice trailed off when she got a closer look at the name tag he wore on his chest. "Oh, Mr. Logan! How nice of you to visit us this morning." She paused when she noticed the oatmeal trailing down the front of his shirt. "Oh dear, our little Mike has been at it again, hasn't he?" She grabbed a tissue out of a box that she held in her hand and began to dab futilely at his shirt.

Who was "our" little Mike? Jeff wondered as he returned the gaze of a glowering inmate. And since they hadn't even been introduced yet, what did the kid have against him?

Jeff looked over the woman's shoulder at a little dark-haired boy whose triumphant smile gave him away. He may have looked as if butter could melt in his mouth, but the evidence of his guilt was dripping down the front of Jeff's shirt.

"Don't bother," Jeff said to the woman, glancing at his shirt. "I can take care of this later."

He smiled politely and glanced at the name tag on her smock. He needed to make friends with the flustered woman so that he could stay and start his way up the learning curve. "Don't worry about the mess, Mrs. Anderson. Luckily, I wore an old shirt."

"Oh, thank you, Mr. Logan," she breathed, glancing around with a worried frown. "I'm afraid you've come at a bad time. Are you here on a tour of inspection?"

"Not at all," he hurried to reassure her. "Maybe I should have called ahead. As I said before, I'm here to volunteer."

When he'd shot off his mouth and told Abby that he would be able to pass a test for fatherhood in thirty days, he hadn't foreseen being doused with oatmeal. Nor dealing with a four-year-old delinquent like "our" Mike. But he was in too deep to back out now.

Visibly relieved, Mrs. Anderson smiled feebly. "Volunteer? For what?"

Jeff could tell that she wasn't convinced he hadn't come to the center to check up on her, and that nothing he could say would make her believe otherwise. There was no help for it. He had to start confiding in her sooner or later in order to get her cooperation. He drew a deep breath and plunged into murky waters. "Actually, I need to gain some experience with small children, including babies."

A blank look came over her face. He didn't blame her. How often would an official of a hotel named after his family show up at its child care center and volunteer to help?

He'd studied hotel management and was currently in charge of supervising the efforts of the staff of the new Logan Wilshire. When he had the place running to his satisfaction, he was slated to move on to another property in Atlanta and start all over again. But what he knew about kids—in any size, shape or form—would fit in a nutshell with room left over. Still, twenty kids shouldn't be that much of a challenge to a man who managed a fifteen-story hotel staffed with hundreds of employees.

"I suppose we *could* find something for you to do," she answered after a few moments of visible soul-searching, "although it's a wee bit out of the ordinary." She gazed at the activity going on around her. "As a matter of fact, we could use some help this morning. Now that we're on daylight savings time," she went on to explain, "the children's systems seem a little put out at having to get up an hour early. Usually, they're not so excitable."

Jeff forced an understanding smile. If she thought the kids' biological systems were upset this morning, it was a good thing she couldn't see the state of his. It didn't take a genius to see that taking care of small children wasn't a game to be taken lightly.

"How can I help you?" he inquired, thankful that she didn't ask any more questions about his wanting to train for fatherhood. He felt like a dimwit—but time was important. He had only thirty days.

Mrs. Anderson motioned to where bowls of hot oatmeal, raisins and brown-sugar topping were being served. "We're shorthanded this morning. If you could help with breakfast, it certainly would be a big help."

He glanced over to the children's tables, where oatmeal seemed to be going north, south, east and west instead of into small mouths. He couldn't understand why no one stopped them. He'd taken on a stint as a dining room manager as part of his hotel management training, and thought he knew the answer. Why didn't these frantic-looking women *organize* the children? Even as his newfound nerves cried for pity, he feared that he was going to have to be a breakfast policeman.

The chief-in-charge took him by the elbow and steered him in the direction of the first table. "Why don't you go over and get started, while I get someone to warm the baby bottles? It usually takes only two of us to supervise breakfast, but today is unusual."

When another glob of oatmeal came sailing toward him and, thankfully, landed on the floor, Jeff had second thoughts about helping with breakfast. "I'm sure the kids are able to feed themselves. All you have to do is show them they have to cooperate to get what they want. All this place needs is a little management."

"Oh, dear!" A pained look creased Mrs. Anderson's forehead. "I just knew you were here to inspect the center. You are, aren't you? Are you going to write us up?"

"Not at all," Jeff answered, thoroughly ashamed of himself. The woman didn't need his criticism; she needed his help. "I came here to help—honest!" He raised his right hand in the Scout salute. "I just thought that if we could shape up the kids, you wouldn't have so much to do. It's the same advice I give to the rest of the hotel staff.''

"The rest of the hotel staff aren't dealing with small children,'' she answered with a frosty look. "Children of this age have minds of their own. Especially children like our Mike.''

Jeff surrendered. If he didn't learn how to be a father in thirty days with Mrs. Anderson to help him, he would be on his own. Only—on his own wasn't where he wanted to be. He wanted to be part of a family.

"I suppose you're right,'' he conceded. "Do you still want me to help the kids with their breakfast?''

"Yes, and you can start with Mike. He's an only child and doesn't take to people readily,'' she whispered. "But maybe he'll bond with you.'' She shot a stern look at the little culprit.

Jeff headed for the nearest table, pulled out a pint-size chair, and traded wary glances with Mike. The boy dipped his spoon into his bowl of oatmeal and stared at Jeff.

"Hi.'' Jeff fixed the kid with a firm look that could have frozen an Eskimo. "My name is Mr. Logan,'' he said. "What's yours?''

The boy clamped his lips shut.

"How about if I help you with your breakfast?'' Jeff asked politely.

The kid, who had obviously been told not to talk to strangers, shook his head. Or maybe he was just being his usual not-so-sweet self.

"How about you?" Jeff asked the child who was sitting next to Mike. He was the boy who had grabbed Mike's wooden train engine and the two had engaged in a mini tug-of-war. Mike had won.

"Are you Batman?" he asked Jeff.

"No, I'm not."

"If you're not Batman, I don't want to talk to you."

The kid's attitude was too much for Jeff. But maybe he could turn it into an educational game. "You're supposed to say 'No, thank you.'"

"What for?"

"Because I asked you if I could help you with your breakfast, that's why." Jeff was trying to be patient, but it didn't look as though he was making any headway.

"I don't like oatmeal!"

"It's good for you," Jeff countered, remembering the words his endless series of nannies had used on him. Then there was that puzzling comment that he would grow if he went to sleep. Maybe the same theory was attached to orange juice. "How about drinking your orange juice? It'll make you grow."

"Don't like that either," the kid answered stubbornly. "'Sides, I'm big enough already."

Mrs. Anderson came to stand beside him, and turned a stern gaze on the table's occupants. "That will be enough," she warned. To Jeff, she added, "Don't worry, Mr. Logan. The children will come around if they see you here often enough."

"I only have thirty mornings," Jeff answered, getting to his feet.

"Thirty mornings to do what?"

Jeff decided to throw himself on her mercy. "I just found out I'm going to be a father. You might say, I need a few pointers."

Mrs. Anderson smiled her relief. "For a few moments I was afraid you were going to put us on probation for thirty days. Will this be your first child?"

"Yes. I figured I better get in training."

"Don't worry. Once you have a child of your own, I daresay fatherhood will come naturally."

"Maybe you think so," he answered, eyeing the miniature adults who were undoubtedly trying to figure out how to get him. "Unfortunately, the baby's mother-to-be is a tough one to convince."

"Wait and see. If the baby isn't here yet, there's no use worrying any more than is necessary," she answered pleasantly. "Now, how would you like to start with the babies?"

Jeff took a deep breath. "Doing…?" He was afraid to come right out and ask exactly what she had in mind, but it didn't matter. He had volunteered to help and he intended to keep his word.

"Come with me. You're just in time to feed the babies and give them a diaper change. That seems like a good place to start."

Jeff stood patiently, taking in the lesson in changing a diaper. "Easy enough," he commented after a few moments.

"I'm glad you think so." Mrs. Anderson smiled. "I'll get the children's bottles and be right back." She gestured to the remaining three cribs that each held a squirming baby, then turned to leave. "You can get started with those three little ones."

"Now, let's see…" Jeff began repeating Mrs. Anderson's instructions out loud. "First you put one hand on the baby's tummy to keep it from squirming out of reach. Then you take off the kid's diaper with your other hand." He smiled down at the mesmerized baby. "Don't worry, kid, I'll have you set to rights in a minute." He was about to reach for the stack of clean diapers when he was hit with a warm stream of water. "Just what I needed." He muttered under his breath, grabbed the old diaper and covered the child to stem another waterfall.

"Thanks a bunch," he muttered. The baby eyed him and screwed up his face. "For Pete's sake, don't cry. They'll think I've done something to hurt you," Jeff muttered. He bent over and looked the baby squarely in the eyes. "I need this job. Now, if you'll just cooperate, we'll try again." To his relief, the kid gave him a toothless grin. Jeff went back to work.

He glanced over his shoulder when he heard a smothered laugh.

"Don't worry, Mr. Logan," Mrs. Anderson announced. "It's a lesson about little boys we all have to learn. The rest of the babies are also boys. Just remember to keep them covered with the old diaper while you change them."

"But I need at least two more hands," he lamented, wiping his hands on the wet soapy towel that she handed him. Then he turned back to the task. "There!" He held the baby up for her inspection, feeling awfully proud of himself.

"There *is* a small problem, Mr. Logan. You've put the diaper on backwards. The tabs close in the front."

"It works for me," he answered grimly.

"You just need a little more practice," she assured him. She handed him the baby and a warm bottle, and pointed to a rocking chair. "You look as if you could use a rest. Why don't you try feeding the baby?"

Jeff wouldn't admit it out loud, but he *did* need a rest. Not only was the job physically draining, but his nerves were shot.

He gazed down at the tiny bundle he held in his arms. One small hand rested on the warm bottle, the other curled around Jeff's fingers. Jeff counted the tiny fingers with its minuscule fingernails, and the tiny toes peeking out of the hand-knit blanket. This was someone's treasured child.

While he rocked the baby to sleep, Jeff envisioned a treasure like this one for his own. Suddenly he could hardly wait to be a dad.

The euphoria lasted throughout the morning. But subsided sometime around lunch. The meal was ham or grilled cheese sandwiches with sliced apples and a small carton of milk. Before Jeff could intercept him, Mike let loose with a barrage of apple slices.

"Okay, fella," Jeff said sternly, hauling the kid out of his chair by his elbow. "Now, pick those up and put them back on the plate."

"Why?"

"Because I said so, that's why." Jeff waited patiently while the kid sized him up. He was banking on the fact that he was bigger.

Mrs. Anderson bustled up. "Any problems?"

"No, ma'am," Jeff answered, forcing a smile in Mike's direction. "Just a slight misunderstanding between us men. Right, Mike?"

Mike straightened his back at Jeff's comment and went to work picking up apple slices.

"See? I told you it was just a matter of the right kind of communication," Jeff said. "Give me some time and I'll have the rest of the kids organized, too."

"Good luck, Mr. Logan. You're going to need it." Mrs. Anderson smothered a laugh as she turned away.

By the time lunch was over, Jeff was sailing along. All the children had been fed and there had been no further episodes with projectile foodstuffs.

As he helped get the kids down on their blankets for nap time, he couldn't help but marvel at his accomplishments. Already he could diaper a baby, warm up a bottle, feed the kid and rock it to sleep. He could even monitor lunchtime without a hitch. And somewhere along the way, he'd even earned Mike's grudging respect by referring to him as a "man." But he realized as the children settled down, he was exhausted.

"I'm afraid I have to leave, Mrs. Anderson," Jeff announced as he checked his watch. "I have to attend to some grown-up business. And, by the way, I'd appreciate your not telling anyone I've been here."

"Not if you don't want me to, Mr. Logan." She beamed. "I must tell you that you're making good progress. Tomorrow, if you like, you can graduate to the older children."

"No more oatmeal?"

"Not tomorrow. As a matter of fact, we try to alternate our menus to keep the children interested. Tomorrow, we're having cold cereal and fresh fruit."

"That sounds pretty safe. There's not much ballistic power in cereal flakes," Jeff said, hoping he would be right. "In that case, I'll be back."

"You might want to read these tonight in preparation for tomorrow." She handed him a pamphlet on child care from infancy to age two. And another on children from two to five. "These will give you a head start on tomorrow. Don't let the contents intimidate you." She eyed him narrowly. "You are coming back tomorrow, aren't you?"

"Yes, but remember, this is our secret."

Back in his suite, Jeff showered and changed into a business suit. The wet and soiled clothing he'd worn that morning went into a laundry chute. Tomorrow he planned to dress appropriately. What did a guy wear on cereal day, anyway?

"ARE YOU SURE ABOUT THIS, Abby?"

The scent of spiced Mexican dishes wafted across the dining room from the restaurant's kitchen. Jeff instantly felt hungry. "I thought you said this type of food upsets your stomach."

"Only when I'm under stress," Abby answered, her face buried in the menu. "Right now, the only stress I'm under is what to order for dinner."

"Drinks, Señor, Señora?"

Abby glanced up at the waiter. "A virgin margarita, *por favor*," she answered.

"Make mine with a double dose of tequila and an extra lime on the side," Jeff replied. "After days like the past few, I need something strong."

The waiter nodded and left for the bar.

"Rough day?" Abby asked. A smile hovered on the corner of her lips as she studied him.

"Days, you mean," he answered. "But I've learned a lot."

Abby studied the menu. "Oh, what have you been doing?"

It was time to come clean and tell Abby what he'd been up to. He proudly said, "Volunteering mornings at the hotel's day care center."

Abby dropped the menu. "You're kidding!"

"Scout's honor." He held up his hand. "I decided I couldn't learn much about kids from reading books, so I took the plunge." He went on to tell her about his adventures. "There's one kid who's taught me a lot about being a father—Mike."

"Really? How old is Mike?"

"Five, going on thirty."

Abby couldn't hide her laughter.

"What could a child of five possibly teach you?"

"That I'm the boss."

Abby let her laughter spill over. "I tried that on Kate when she was five, but it didn't always work."

Jeff grinned. "Mike and I have reached an understanding. I'm the boss of the outfit, and he's my helper. It makes him feel important and keeps him out of trouble."

"Whatever works, I guess," Abby commented, and went back to deciding what to order.

Jeff added the juice of the lime to the margarita that the waiter served. "As soon as I get my diploma from the day care center, I'll provide you with all the answers about fatherhood you care to ask."

Abby peered around the menu.

"Diploma? From a day care center? You're joking, right?"

"Nope. How else can I prove to you I've passed the curriculum on the care and feeding of small children? When you get to know me better, you'll find I never do things halfway, Abby, and I never give up easily." He gave her a theatrical leer.

Abby returned the lopsided grin that so enchanted her. Jeff was funny when circumstances called for humor, and played it straight when they didn't. Right now, affection shone in his eyes and in his voice as he regarded her across the table. How could he be so sexy when he was discussing a stint in a day care center?

If she hadn't already fallen in love with him, the tender look in his eyes, combined with his sense of humor, would have pushed her over the edge.

"So, how are the arrangements for Kate's wedding coming along?"

"Fine, thank goodness," Abby answered, dipping a nacho chip into a bowl of guacamole sauce seasoned with dried red peppers. "Since Kate wanted a simple wedding, we're almost ready. I made arrangements for a caterer this morning."

Jeff frowned.

"I didn't realize you were moving so fast or I would have spoken up earlier. I was going to offer one of the hotel's dining rooms for the reception as my wedding present to Kate and Sebastian. And, by the way, I'm not sure what you're eating is good for you."

Abby shook her head and smiled. "Relax. As for a wedding reception, I couldn't possibly accept such a gift. And I'm sure Kate and Sebastian feel the same way."

"Why not? After all," he added as if a thought struck him, "I'm going to be her stepfather." He said it confidently, as if he would tolerate no argument from Abby about marrying him.

"Kate's stepfather," she repeated slowly. "Stepfather to a twenty-one-year-old woman?"

"Yeah," he answered with that wicked grin of his. "And Sebastian's stepfather-in-law."

Abby dropped the chip into the guacamole dip. She reached for her drink, tasted it and grimaced. What she needed at the moment was something a lot stronger than what amounted to fruit juice and ginger ale. She'd barely come to terms with thinking of Sebastian as her son-in-law, but she hadn't taken the time to think of Jeff as Sebastian's father-in-law.

"Good heavens!" She stared at Jeff as if she were seeing him for the first time. "Now that you put it that way, can't you see how the whole idea of our getting married sounds utterly ridiculous?"

"It's not ridiculous, Abby," he answered. He reached across the table and took her hand in his. "This baby of ours is real. And so is the idea of your marrying me."

The waiter arrived with Abby's chicken tostada and Jeff's steak and bean burrito. The sight of the sour cream and guacamole topping on her salad, coupled with Jeff's pronouncement about his possible future relationship to her family, sent her stomach into a tailspin and the rest of her into another episode of giggles.

Jeff as Kate's stepfather?

Jeff as Sebastian's father-in-law?

Jeff as a grandfather?

Abby covered her face with her napkin and gave vent to her reaction.

"Abby, you're crying!" Jeff jumped up and rushed around the table to put a glass of ice water to her lips. "Here, drink this. I knew I shouldn't have brought you here."

"Stop, you're drowning me!" Abby gasped, still laughing. "I'm not crying. I'm laughing."

"Laughing? At what?"

"Just think of it," she explained when she could catch her breath. "If we married, what would your relationship to Kate and *her* children be? Let alone to Sebastian?"

Jeff resumed his seat and tried to follow Abby's train of thought. It wasn't easy to concentrate on family trees with Abby looking so delectable and so close.

"When we get married, I suppose I'll be...their grandfather!" He sat back in his chair and looked surprised. "Kind of scary, isn't it?"

Abby wiped her eyes and agreed. "*If* we get married. I'm not so sure all of this talk about marriage is a good idea, after all. The whole idea boggles the imagination."

"I've never taken the time to think about it before now," Jeff agreed, "but I suppose you're right. It will raise a lot of eyebrows." He burst into a broad smile. "Hey, I just might get into the *Guinness Book of Records* as the world's youngest grandfather."

"And that doesn't bother you?"

"No. I always wished I came from a large family, with several sisters and brothers to play with. It would have made having our parents away so much easier for my sister and me to handle." He smiled a wistful smile that started to melt some of Abby's misgivings. "Marrying you is the nicest way to acquire a family that I can think of."

She held the glass of ice water to her hot cheek. "You can't begin to know how I feel about your being a grandfather to Kate's children. And no matter how you sugarcoat it, I'm pretty sure I know how people are going to react to seeing us together. Especially after Patrick is born. They'll probably think I'm robbing the cradle at the same time that I'm filling it. Maybe we ought to keep this quiet and not tell anyone you're the father."

"Abby," he protested, "I may not know much about babies, but I do know that pretty soon you won't be able to hide Patrick. As for not telling anyone I'm his father, why not?"

There was no way around it. Abby knew she had to tell him the way she felt.

"I'm too old for you."

"Come on, you're not that much older than I am. Besides, if anyone is stupid enough to say anything, I'll be the first to tell them you're the best thing that ever happened to me. Quit worrying over it."

Abby shook her head. "I'm not as confident as you are." She sighed. "As for having a baby now, it's been twenty-one years since I had Kate. So many things have changed."

"Not to worry. By the time the baby arrives, I'll be a pro," he assured her. "And just remember, this time around you have *me*. I'll be there to help. For keeps. As for what people might think about us, they're going to envy me."

"I know you're serious about all of this," Abby answered, smiling, "but being a father is more than reading books and changing diapers. Or even volunteering at a child care center. As a matter of fact," she added with a quizzical grin at Jeff's serious demeanor, "I wonder if you'd actually realize what you'd be letting yourself in for if I actually took you seriously and agreed to marry you."

"Oh, I do. And you'd better get started taking me seriously, Abby Carson," Jeff said. "Because when my stint at the center is over, you *are* going to marry me."

Chapter Ten

After browsing through the Family section of his local bookstore, Jeff began to understand what Abby had meant about what he was letting himself in for. Not even the pamphlets Mrs. Anderson had given him had provided such challenging detail. But he'd made a deal and, come hell or high water, he intended to stick by it.

He paid for his purchases and headed for Abby's office.

"Getting to be a regular visitor around here, aren't you?" Nadine teased with a welcoming smile.

Jeff returned her grin. "You could say so."

She eyed the small shopping bag with the Barnes & Noble bookstore logo.

"Shopping?"

"Sort of." Although common sense told him that there was no way she could possibly know what was in the bag, he'd learned never to underestimate a woman. Especially one like Nadine.

He'd been so intent on wanting to show Abby his

purchases that he'd overlooked having to pass Nadine's good-natured scrutiny.

She was obviously a pro at ferreting out information she wanted, but she wasn't going to get anything out of him if he could help it.

"Coffee?"

"Er—no thanks," Jeff replied. The last time he'd enjoyed Nadine's hospitality, it had taken two days to get over the shock to his system. "A cookie would be nice," he said to placate her. "I was hoping Abby had come in."

"Any minute now," Nadine answered. She handed him a cookie without taking her eyes off his shopping bag. "So, what brings you here today?"

He searched for an answer that would satisfy her.

Nadine was bound to know he'd already put a deposit on the Westwood house. And, unless he was wrong about Abby's mother, he was sure Caroline must have told Nadine that he and Abby had spent the weekend together.

"Just visiting," he said weakly. Good God, he thought, what was there about the woman's piercing eyes that made him feel as if he were five years old with the truth written on his forehead?

Nadine regarded him knowingly. "You don't say. In that case, you might as well have a seat. Sure you don't want some coffee to go with that? I just brewed a fresh pot."

He was saved from answering when Abby came through the door.

Abby looked so pleased to see him that his

thoughts turned instinctively to the last time they
were together, a few nights ago. Just thinking of
their foray into the hotel kitchen for chocolate cake
and ice cream—and what came after—made him
want to grab her again and never let go. But not in
front of the nosy Nadine. He got himself under control.

"I was on my way to the hotel, but I stopped in
to show you something."

When they were safely behind closed doors, Jeff
emptied the shopping bag on Abby's desk.

She picked up *Dr. Spock's Baby and Childcare*
book and the one for expectant fathers, then looked
at Jeff in amazement.

"I decided practical experience isn't enough for
fatherhood. For starters, look at this one." Jeff
opened the guidebook for expectant fathers and
pointed to a paragraph he'd outlined with a yellow
marker. "It clearly says I should be involved from
day one."

Abby laughed helplessly and dropped into a chair.
"You're not actually going to go through with this,
are you?"

"Sure," he answered, turning the pages. "I've
never been so serious about anything in my life.
Look, it says here I should talk to your doctor. How
about calling and getting us an appointment?"

Abby held up her hands. "Not on your life. If
you want to study those books, go ahead. But I draw
the line at anything else. Besides, I have Kate's wedding arrangements to keep me busy."

KATE MAY HAVE WANTED a small, intimate wedding, but this wasn't it. Jeff got his first hint when he arrived at Kate's wedding and found the little church almost full.

Directed to a pew on the bride's side of the aisle, he gazed around him. The church was small but impressive. The setting sun shining through the stained-glass windows behind the pulpit created multicolored light beams. The scent of flowers in white baskets surrounding the pulpit filled the air. Rows of worn mahogany pews were festooned with white satin ribbon. Soft music played in the background.

The thought that he might soon be standing at the altar himself was intimidating. On the other hand, he mused, second weddings probably were different. And with Abby as the bride, he could face anything.

He found himself hoping Abby would seriously accept his proposal, and looking forward to the day he and Abby would tie the knot. He wished it could be soon.

At the moment, he felt as if today's wedding guests were eyeing him, wondering who he was and what he was doing here. He wasn't old enough to be Sebastian's contemporary. And he considered himself too old to be Kate's. He could almost hear minds whirling with questions.

"Kate is a beautiful bride, isn't she?" The question broke into his thoughts. It was from Nadine, who, undetected by him, had squeezed her way into the pew to sit beside him. Nadine gestured to where

Kate waited at the door for the *Wedding March* to begin.

"Yes, she is," Jeff agreed. But his eyes were on Abby, who was making her way to the front pew. She looked spectacular. "And the miracle of it is that she's going to belong to me."

Nadine's laugh brought him up short.

"Something funny?"

"Not a thing, except that I was referring to Kate, not to her mother. As for Abby, the two of you are beginning to act as moonstruck as Kate and Sebastian."

Nadine suddenly got his full attention. "Is it that obvious?"

"At least to me. I don't know about everyone else. From what I've seen, you might as well get on with asking Abby to marry you."

Jeff couldn't bring himself to tell Nadine that he'd already asked Abby, and that he was waiting for her to make up her mind. The information would only lead to questions he wasn't prepared to answer.

"In case you're wondering how to go about getting Abby to marry you," Nadine went on, "courting a woman is kind of like playing baseball."

"Baseball?" Jeff's eyes widened at the analogy.

"Sure, it is. You connect with the ball—that'll be Abby, you understand—and head for first base. From the way Abby has been looking at you, my guess is that you've probably already accomplished that much."

Fascinated, he raised his eyebrows. He wasn't the kind of guy to kiss and tell.

"The trick then, Mr. Logan, is to steal your way to second base before Abby notices it. In this case, second base being Abby's heart. But," she added with a wicked grin, "I'd guess you've gone that far already, too."

Jeff ignored her remark. "And third base?"

"That's the best part of all," Nadine answered smugly. "When you get to third base, you grab Abby by the arm and run like hell to the nearest preacher—that being home plate."

Jeff mulled over Nadine's unorthodox description of courting. He wasn't all that knowledgeable about women—or baseball, for that matter—but she might be right at that. By some happy miracle, he'd unexpectedly reached first base without a major problem, and had already talked his way to second—with some success, he thought fondly. His problem now was getting to third base by convincing Abby he was ready, willing and able to be a husband and a father so they could head for home together.

If Abby's reluctance to marry him was based on her thinking he didn't want a wife and children, she was mistaken. He had never before found the right woman to start a family with.

He was positive Abby loved him. But their temporary truce aside, the million-dollar question was this: Did she love him enough to marry him?

At the moment, Jeff felt bone-weary. Weeks of giving up his mornings to volunteer at the hotel's day care center were playing havoc with his physical stamina, let alone his duties as manager at the Wilshire. He had only a few more days to go at the day care center, but he'd worn himself out with fancy footwork to stay out of trouble before trouble caught up with him.

At the rate he was going, there'd be hell to pay if his father got wind of what he'd been up to.

The opening strains of the *Wedding March* sounded. In her white silk and lace wedding gown, her face glowing with happiness, Kate made her way down the aisle on her father's arm. Sebastian, waiting at the altar, looked bewitched by his young bride. Richard seemed to have come to grips with the idea of Kate marrying a man his own age; he was beaming with pride.

But Abby—the woman he hoped to make his bride—was in a class by herself.

Seated in a front pew along with Caroline, Abby looked radiant in a pink silk suit with a matching hat. Her face shone with a serene inner happiness only a self-assured, mature woman could feel at her daughter's wedding. He could see her enchanting blue-green eyes sparkle when she turned to watch Kate walk down the aisle.

From the broadening of her smile when their eyes met briefly, he sensed Abby was as aware of him as he was of her.

He couldn't take his eyes off her. As far as he was concerned, there wasn't a more beautiful woman in the church than Abby. Not even the bride.

He considered himself a very lucky man. If he weren't already in love with Abby, he thought happily, he would have tumbled head over heels in love with her tonight. For no one else but her would he have put his reputation as a sane man on the line by volunteering at a child care center.

He only hoped his reputation as the manager of the Logan Wilshire hadn't gone to hell in a handbasket in the process.

The pause in the marriage ceremony finally registered. He turned his attention to the pulpit, or to be more accurate, to Abby. Maybe, just maybe, he thought as he noticed the soft smile that curved her lips, today's wedding had put her in a romantic mood. Maybe now was the time to ask her again to marry him.

"I now pronounce you man and wife." The minister beamed at the newlyweds and closed his prayer book. "You may kiss the bride."

"Family and friends," the cleric went on after Sebastian placed a gentle kiss on Kate's lips, "I have the pleasure of introducing Katherine and Sebastian to you for the first time as Mr. and Mrs. Sebastian Curtis!"

The audience erupted in applause. The bride and groom marched up the aisle to good-natured comments.

Abby, wiping tears from the corners of her eyes, followed on her ex-husband's arm.

Jeff gazed after Abby. He'd never cared for her as much as he did today. Not even when he'd suggested that they get married. But never, he realized as if a bolt of lightning had struck him, had he actually told her how much he loved her!

Instead, once he'd found out about the baby, he'd tried to convince Abby to marry him so Patrick could have a live-in father. Big mistake.

He should have told Abby he'd fallen for her the first moment he'd laid eyes on her. That he'd come to love her and wanted to marry her for her simple honesty, her caring ways, her pragmatic approach to life that complemented his own casual style. He should have told her Patrick was just the icing on the cake.

He caught up with the bridal party in the social hall adjoining the church, where they were accepting congratulations inside the door. In the hall, recorded music was playing the latest love song.

Weddings were romantic. Even Jeff could see that. It didn't help to know that Abby had been married in the same church. The smile Richard kept directing to Abby was a dead giveaway that the man was still in love with her. Jeff was afraid the romantic scenario was just what Richard needed to ask Abby to marry him again.

Jeff knew he had to move fast. He had to tell Abby how much he loved her. He had to make her understand *he* was the man who belonged in her life.

With the guests milling around the social hall, third base seemed tantalizingly out of reach.

It wasn't until the newlyweds were about to cut

the wedding cake that he got the chance to speak to Abby.

Her smile broadened when she saw him approach. He had been on her mind all through the wedding ceremony.

"It was a beautiful wedding, Abby," Jeff said when he took her hand. He glanced at the line of guests behind him. "Do you suppose we could find somewhere to talk? I have something important to tell you."

"Now?" she answered, waving at a friend's greeting. "Can you wait until later?"

"No. I've waited too long as it is."

The serious look on his face registered through Abby's happiness. "Too long? Why? Is something wrong?"

"Sort of, and I intend to take care of it as soon as I can."

"I'm sorry. I can't get away tonight," Abby said reluctantly. "There's still the cake cutting, and I promised Kate I would help her change for her honeymoon. She and Sebastian have decided to drive up the coast for a few days."

She saw a shadow pass over Jeff's face. "I'm sorry—I really am. Can it wait until tomorrow?"

Jeff nodded reluctantly. "I suppose it'll have to."

"Champagne, Abby?"

"No, I can't—" It wasn't a waiter, but Richard offering her a fluted glass. The questioning look in her ex-husband's eyes stopped her. How could she turn down champagne on the night of her daughter's wedding without raising suspicions?

"On second thought, yes, thank you," she answered. She accepted the champagne and raised it in salute. "Did you bring a glass for Jeff?"

"No, sorry," Richard said with a casual shrug. "Didn't think of it."

Gazing at the expressions on their faces as they looked at each other, Abby saw once again that there was some sort of polite rivalry going on between the two men. Somehow she had to make them understand that there was room in her life for both of them, and that she wasn't prepared to make a choice. But not tonight. Tonight she was the mother of the bride.

"Can't we talk about this tomorrow morning?" she asked Jeff. "Kate and Sebastian are about to cut the wedding cake."

"I have something going on in the morning," he answered vaguely. "Maybe some other time."

"What's going on?" Richard gazed thoughtfully at Jeff.

"I was about to tell Abby about a field trip I planned for tomorrow."

"A field trip?" Richard grinned. "Sounds like the good old days. I didn't realize you were still in school."

Abby froze at the obvious reference to the age difference between herself and Jeff. The reminder was the last thing she wanted to hear at a happy time like this. She glanced at the guests. Did anyone suspect her relationship with Jeff? Did her friends share Richard's amusement?

The tension was thick enough to cut with a knife, Abby thought as she hurriedly handed her former husband her untouched glass of champagne. "Why don't we all go and get a piece of wedding cake?"

JEFF WAS HAVING a great time getting the kids ready. The field trip he'd promised them this last morning of his volunteering stint was sort of a farewell present. If only Abby were here, the day would be perfect.

Last night at the wedding, he'd intended to invite her for his "graduation" ceremony. Too bad Abby's ex had stuck to her like glue, making it impossible for Jeff to get her alone. But at least a sympathetic Mrs. Anderson promised him a mock diploma to show Abby.

Just when he'd resolved himself to not having Abby here, the center door opened and in she walked.

A tidal wave of noise swept over Abby when she opened the door. A group of children between the ages of three and five milled around the room, shouting that they were ready.

Ready for what? Abby wondered as she came in.

"Abby?" A broad smile broke over Jeff's face when he spotted her. "I was just hoping for a miracle and here you are! How did you know where to find me?"

Abby made her way to his side. "I called the

hotel and they told me you were here. Actually, I wanted to apologize for not being able to talk to you last night. I hope I'm not in the way.''

"Not at all," Jeff answered happily. "We're about to take a field trip. Want to come along?''

Abby nodded. "I'm a pro at field trips," she answered. "Where's this one going?''

Before he could reply, Mrs. Anderson joined him.

"I'm so sorry, Mr. Logan," she said. "You'll have to excuse the children. This is their first field trip and they're naturally excited at the idea." She handed him a sheaf of papers. "These are the permission slips signed by the children's parents.''

Permission slips? That was a new one on him. One more item of information to store away in his mental training-for-fatherhood manual. "Thank you. Mrs. Anderson, I'd like you to meet Abby Carson. She's going to come along with us.''

"How nice to meet you, my dear." Mrs. Anderson cocked her head and smiled at Abby. "I feel as though I know you.''

Abby was surprised. She managed a smile of her own as she took the woman's hand. "I'm sorry. This *is* the first time we've met, isn't it?''

"Yes, of course." Mrs. Anderson beamed at her. "It's just that from what Mr. Logan has said about you and the baby you both are expecting, I felt as though I know you." She stopped when she noticed Abby's surprised reaction. "Oh dear, you are the mother, aren't you?" she asked.

Hovering on the point of embarrassment, Abby nodded. After all, surrounded by children and babies, she figured this was a perfectly natural place to admit her pregnancy. And from the way the children were happily massed around Jeff, it seemed equally natural for him to be a father-to-be.

"By the way, I can't tell you how wonderful Mr. Logan has been, both with his help and his ideas," Mrs. Anderson went on. "We certainly are indebted to him."

Jeff shifted restlessly. "I haven't done that much," he muttered. "Just applied a few management techniques to the job. Now, how about if we get the show on the road. We have to be in and out of the kitchens before lunch preparations begin."

"A kitchen?" Abby asked through the confusion. "I thought you said you were going on a field trip?"

"We are," Jeff assured her. "We're going to tour the hotel's kitchens. And we're going to bake cookies, too."

"You have to be joking," Abby said, noticing the difficulty the two helpers were having lining up the excited children. She shouldn't have been that surprised, she mused—not when Jeff had been coming up with all sorts of surprising ideas lately.

She had visions of dozens of little hands mixing ingredients, flour flying in the air, and more chocolate chips eaten than were baked in cookies. Making cookies with one child had presented a challenge—but fourteen?

"No problem," Jeff answered. "We've been

practicing with play dough.'' He raised his voice. "Okay, kids, pick a partner and get in line. Mike, you can be the monitor at the front of the line. Wally, you take up at the end.''

Abby watched the children choose a partner and get in an uneven line in front of Jeff. Seeing the way the children responded to Jeff made the edges of Abby's heart begin to melt. She traded an incredulous look with Mrs. Anderson.

"It's almost a miracle, the way they respond to Mr. Logan, isn't it?'' Mrs. Anderson said under her breath. "He's even gotten two of the most difficult children to behave. All the children love him. He says it's a matter of proper communication and instilling a sense of pride and responsibility in the children.''

"On small children like these?''

"It seems to work.'' Mrs. Anderson laughed softly at Abby's reaction. "I suppose children are smarter than we give them credit for. Or better still, perhaps Mr. Logan is wiser than he gave himself credit for. You take Mike over there.'' She indicated a small dark-haired boy standing proudly at the head of the line. "He was a terror until your Mr. Logan had a talk with him about responsibility. And Wally, too. Now, look at them.''

Abby looked at a proud Mike and Wally and at "her'' Mr. Logan. For a man who'd said he'd never been around small children, he was a fast learner. And she had clearly underestimated him.

Abby's heart melted a little more. If this kept up,

she'd be throwing herself into Jeff's arms and asking him to marry her.

Jeff handed out badges with each child's name printed in large red letters.

"Now remember, everyone, we have to be quiet as mice while we go through the lobby. Got it? Mrs. Anderson?" he added when fourteen little heads nodded in unison. "What do you say we get started?"

"Right away." She exchanged a pleased smile with Abby. "Mrs. Carson and I will follow you."

"Here we go." Jeff led the way out the door.

Abby found herself proud of the group as they crossed the hotel lobby. She was prouder still when she noted the surprised glances, smiles and nods of approval that followed them as they trooped to the service elevators. Whatever magic Jeff had employed to charm the children, it was working. Even on her.

One thing was clear, he knew more about human nature, young or old, than she'd ever have guessed. Maybe he *was* ready to be a father.

The large kitchen, with a smaller one beyond it where breakfast preparations were still in process, gleamed with polished stainless-steel working surfaces. Copper pots and pans hung from racks and covered the stoves. Fresh fruits and vegetables were being brought out from large walk-in refrigerators. The scent of spices filled the air.

Wolfgang, the daytime chef-in-charge, greeted them when they arrived. "Ah, Mr. Logan. I see you're right on time and that you've brought our future chefs with you.'' He beamed at the awed children. ''First, I've arranged to show you our kitchens. Then we're going to learn how to make cookies.'' He paused for effect. ''Chocolate chip cookies!''

The children squealed with glee.

''I've asked two of the assistants to Albert, our pastry chef, to help with the baking lesson,'' the chef went on. ''Are you all ready?''

Future chefs? Abby smiled when the children preened. This wasn't just an ordinary field trip, she realized, but an exercise in self-esteem.

''Good. Now, for the tour. This way, please.''

She was even more impressed when the children, with clenched hands at their sides, silently made their way past mounds of fresh food waiting to be prepared for lunch. Eventually, the chef led them to a separate area in a corner that had been set up for them.

Small stools and tables borrowed from the child care center were waiting, along with clean, white aprons. Ingredients, measuring cups and bowls were at each setting. Aluminum cookie sheets were lined up in the center of the table. More of Jeff's planning, she assumed.

She helped to hang the aprons around the children's necks, then tied the surplus fabric out of the way. Together with the class, she watched as the two assistant pastry chefs demonstrated, step by step, how to put ingredients together.

"Having fun, Abby?" Jeff grinned at her from across the table.

His hands sticky with cookie dough, Jeff looked so youthful and so pleased with himself that he made Abby feel young again, too.

The kitchen, with dozens of busy people surrounding her, was the last place she'd expected to be reminded of Jeff's glances, his sensuous hands on her skin, his lips on hers, his bare skin against her bare skin. How could she be so aware of him in the middle of a cooking lesson?

Maybe it was his smile when he joked around with the children. Maybe it was the realization that his heart was in tune with the fourteen small souls. Maybe it was because he was behaving more like a father than Richard had ever done.

Whatever it was about Jeff that got to her, his attraction was all there. And so was her revised opinion of his potential for fatherhood.

She'd decided long ago that if she ever remarried, it would be for love—a word that described her current blind, hungry, tender feeling for Jeff. She wanted him with an ache that grew every time she saw him. So much so that she was going to tell him "yes" as soon as the thirty-day trial period was over. She wished it were tomorrow.

"How did you like the field trip, Abby?"

Shaken out of her reverie, Abby met Jeff's eyes before she gazed around the kitchen. The cooking lesson appeared to be over. The scent of baking chocolate chip cookies filled the air. The children were lined up at a stainless-steel sink, washing their hands under Mrs. Anderson's guidance.

Abby returned Jeff's warm gaze. "More than you know," she answered.

He handed her a heart-shaped cookie that he'd made. "Will you take this—and my heart with it?"

"Yes," Abby whispered, even as she wondered whether what she felt for Jeff was enough to base a marriage on.

"No more doubts?"

"Maybe," she answered, running a fingertip over the raw cookie. It was the first chocolate chip heart she'd ever seen. "But somehow they don't seem so important anymore."

"Good, because after this is over, I'd like us to go upstairs so I can tell you what I started to at Kate's wedding."

Abby's mind flashed back to the scene during which Jeff had asked to speak with her. His eyes had telegraphed a longing that had kept her awake long into the night. That same longing was sweeping through her now. "You'll have to make it short," she answered with a sigh. "I have a one o'clock appointment with a client."

"Abby," he said, lightly brushing his knuckles over her flushed cheek. "When are you going to stop running around in circles and take some time for yourself?"

"Soon, I hope. In the meantime, I have to have a reason for getting up in the morning."

"How about me?" Jeff asked. His gaze fanned

the heat running through her. "Wouldn't I be enough reason?"

Two minds with a single thought, Abby thought when her heart waltzed at his question. "Maybe," she teased. "It all depends."

"On what?"

"First, you'll have to finish whatever it was you started," she answered. His eyes lit up. So did the fire in her middle.

"Is that all?" he said, running a finger over her lips. "Come with me after this, and I'll show you."

"Jeff!" Abby whispered. "Remember we're in plain sight of everyone in the kitchen."

"No one's paying any attention to us," he answered. He bent over and kissed her lightly on the lips. "The rest of what I wanted to show you can wait until we're alone."

The nerve endings in Abby's body quivered. The heat in the kitchen's ovens was nothing compared to the one in her heart. What was there about a kiss in the hotel kitchen that invited emotions like this? she wondered. Was it because kitchens and the scent of food cooking spoke of home, hearth and family?

"I wish I could stay with you, but I have a client who's very anxious to make an offer. He's depending on me to meet him this afternoon."

Jeff nodded. "Later, then?" His sultry gaze turned to one of speculation. "How do you feel about baseball?"

"Baseball?" It was the last subject Abby expected Jeff to mention at such an intimate moment.

"It's all right, I suppose. Actually, I've never been a real fan of the game. Why do you want to know?"

"Because the season's opener is next Saturday. The Logan Corporation has a permanent VIP box at the stadium." He rubbed at his chin as he studied her. When he dropped his hand, he'd left a smudge of chocolate behind that made him even more endearing to her.

"And you want me to go with you?" Abby asked absently, her eyes on the streak of chocolate at the side of his lips. She fought the temptation to kiss it away.

"Why not?"

Abby couldn't think of one reason why she shouldn't go with him, although she would have preferred a more intimate setting for their conversation. "Okay."

"Great," he answered with a wry smile. "I need to do some research."

"Research at a ball game? Is it for a story you're writing?"

"You might say so," Jeff replied with a wry smile. "I need to come up with an ending."

Chapter Eleven

"What's going on in here?" a familiar voice boomed across the kitchen. "Who are these children?"

Jeff froze. His father! It was the last voice he expected or wanted to hear.

Glowering, his father appeared in front of the swinging doors. Behind him, Jeff's sister Elaine threw up her hands and rolled her eyes heavenward. It didn't take much for Jeff to realize trouble had finally caught up with him.

"Dad? What are you doing here?"

With a sinking feeling, Jeff realized the day of reckoning had arrived sooner than he'd expected. He glanced at the startled expression on Abby's face. Maybe sooner wasn't better after all.

At the sound of the man's gruff voice and the anger on his face, Abby's euphoria vanished. From the graying brown hair, brandy-colored eyes and physical resemblance, the man was obviously Jeff's father. The heart-shaped cookie dough that Jeff had made for her dropped from her hand and landed on the floor in an unidentifiable glob.

All the earlier misgivings she'd had over Jeff's relationship with his father instinctively resurfaced. Coupled with Jeff's indecision about a choice of career and her misgivings about the difference in their ages, her own insecurities about her relationship with Jeff assailed her.

Her stomach clenched in knots. Instinctively, she reached for a paper towel from the stack on the table, and put it to her lips.

Jeff glanced at Abby. When he saw the look of dismay on her face, he shot a warning glance at his father and moved to her side. He put a reassuring arm around her and squeezed her shoulder gently.

"The children are from the hotel employees' day care center, Dad," Jeff told his father. "We're on a field trip. Hold up while I have them taken back. We can talk later," he warned before his father could resume his tirade. He motioned to Mrs. Anderson. "Do you mind taking the children back to the center? Don't worry about the cookies, I'll have someone bring them down as soon as they're ready."

"Cookies? Good God, Jeffrey!" his father thundered, his face mottled with anger. "Don't you realize the position you've put us in? What if one of the children hurt themselves here? Our insurance undoubtedly doesn't even cover such a fool stunt as this!" He paused to glare at Jeff. "In spite of all the time and trouble I've taken to interest you in the

management of the hotels, you've never taken me
seriously. And now—this!''

Jeff put a warning finger to his lips and motioned
to a hovering busboy. "Pete, please see Mrs. Anderson and the children get down to the day care
center.''

When the subdued children had filed out the door,
Jeff motioned for everyone to get back to work. He
turned back to face his livid father.

"Abby, this is my father and my sister. Dad,
Elaine, I'd like you to meet Abby Carson.''

"I'm pleased to meet you,'' Abby answered quietly, her insides churning. What had started as a
lighthearted field trip had turned into a nightmare,
and stolen her happiness. She was tempted to leave,
but someone had to support Jeff.

From the unhappy way Jeff's sister was regarding
her brother, Abby sensed a sympathetic soul. She
was sure that she could count on Elaine to support
her brother. Jeff's father, in his present state of
mind, was another story.

Her heart went out to Jeff. He didn't deserve his
father's anger, or the insinuation that Jeff was a failure. If the man had taken the time to get to know
his son, surely he would have seen and admired
Jeff's rapport with the hotel staff. And the way
everyone, including the children, related to him.

As far as she could tell, Jeff's only failure in the
whole situation had been to avoid coming to terms
with his father.

Elaine Logan edged her way around her father

and came to Abby's side. "I'm sorry you had to hear this, Abby," she said quietly. "I'm sure my father is, too, aren't you, Dad?" The tone of her voice left no room for argument.

"Perhaps this meeting *is* unfortunate, Ms. Carson." Jeff's father glanced at the last of the departing children and reluctantly agreed. "I was told my son was in the kitchens. I assumed he was attending to hotel business. The sight of all those children in here took me by surprise." He hesitated, and glanced around before he went on. "I suppose I could have chosen a better time and place, but there's no doubt in my mind that Jeff has made a grave error in bringing anyone into the kitchens who doesn't belong here."

It may not have been the wisest choice for a field trip, Abby privately agreed, but Jeff had taken great pains to ensure the safety of the children. She was tempted to tell Mr. Logan that he owed Jeff an apology, too. That is, if she could call his father's comments to her an apology. But the set look on Jeff's face told her that he was able to hold his own.

"There has to be room for something more than the kind of work you're talking about, Dad. We're dealing with people," Jeff said quietly. "The kids and I were learning something from each other."

"What could those children possibly teach you that I haven't been able to teach you?" his father demanded.

"How to live in each other's world, for one thing," Jeff replied. "I've been working with them, and they've taught me a number of things. Not only that, but their parents work here. I thought the kids needed to have an appreciation of what their parents do for a living. I wanted to thank the kids and give them an experience to remember.''

His father snorted. ''What makes your world so different from the one I planned for you?''

''That's the problem, Dad. It's always been *your* work and *your* plans for me—never mine,'' Jeff answered. ''You want me to live in your structured business world where everything is dollars and cents. I've tried, but I still want to take risks on a dream I've had for more years than I can remember.''

He glanced over at Abby's pale face. ''I don't think this is the time or the place to discuss the differences between us. As for me, I've explained myself to you as much as I know how. Now, it's up to you to try to understand. I'm willing to discuss this, but not here. I'm going to take Abby home first.''

With a final glance behind him at his father's still angry face, Jeff took Abby's hand and led her out of the kitchen and into an adjoining dining room where a few hotel guests still lingered over breakfast. ''I'm so sorry Dad blew up with you around, Abby. I'll make it up to you, I promise.'' He pulled out a chair. ''Here, sit down and wait a minute while I apologize to Wolfgang for my father's behavior.''

He headed for the swinging doors into the kitchen. His father and sister were deep in conversation with the chef. The kitchen crew was busy trying to behave as if nothing had happened. But something had happened all right, Jeff reflected. The way he saw it, he and his father had finally come to a parting of the ways. No more trying to spare his father at his own expense.

Maybe his father was right about one thing. Maybe he needed to make up his own mind about the future. By waiting to make his father understand his own choice for a career, he'd only made matters worse. Thank goodness Elaine would be there to take over when he finally made the break.

But he would have given anything for the inevitable blowup not to have happened in front of Abby.

In the dining room, Abby held a shaking hand to her forehead and relived the scene she'd witnessed, but not willingly. It had made such a deep impression on her that she couldn't put it out of her mind. To her growing dismay, it was as if she were looking into a mirror. She recognized a part of Jeff's father in her.

Even though she'd found much to admire, and even to love, about Jeff, she'd still expected him to change for her. To become her idea of what a husband and father should be. To choose work at a profession that *she* felt spelled security instead of trying to make a career as a writer. She'd wanted him to stop taking risks with his future for her sake. To put away his dreams for hers. And in the process—heaven help them both—she'd inadvertently made him pay for her ex-husband's failure as a husband and father.

Jeff's wealthy background hadn't given her the sense of security she needed. It was the uncertainty of never knowing what he might want to do next that bothered her.

He'd tried beyond her expectations—she was willing to give him that. Who else but a loving and caring man would have studied books on child development and volunteered at a day care center to prove that he could turn into the man she wanted him to be?

She began to realize that it wasn't fair to try to change his basic nature, and that if she did decide to marry him, such a marriage couldn't possibly last. She loved Jeff too much to keep on insisting he change into the man she wanted him to be.

In her own way, she was no better than Jeff's father. Even if she couldn't bring herself to live with Jeff's dream, she owed him his freedom to dream. To become the writer he wanted to be. Even if it broke her heart, she had to somehow cut the ties between them without making him feel guilty. For his sake, and because she loved him—

Her heart ached as she finally realized what she'd done to him.

"Abby? Are you okay?"

"Some," she answered. She steeled herself to do the right thing.

"Want to talk?" Jeff asked cautiously. "I have a feeling we have some unfinished business. So what do you say we get it over with and pretend this never happened.''

"No, I don't think I can. Enough has been said for now," she replied sadly. "I'd rather go home now."

"Are you sure, Abby?"

"I'm sure," she answered. "There's no point in rehashing this morning. It's over."

"If you can wait a few minutes while I call upstairs, I'll take you home. The way you look, I'd rather not let you leave by yourself."

"No, I'd rather you didn't come with me," Abby said woodenly. "I came in a cab and I can take another one home."

The set look on Abby's face sent chills of foreboding through Jeff. Something told him that this was more than a goodbye. "What exactly are you trying to tell me, Abby?"

"That we're better off not seeing each other—at least until the baby is born."

Thunderstruck, Jeff grabbed her arm. "Hold on, Abby. After all we've been through together, you can't possibly mean that. Patrick isn't due for another five months!"

"I'm afraid I do," Abby replied. Her heart was breaking, but, she thought sadly, it was better to break her own than his. If she couldn't change her own nature, she had no right to expect him to change his.

"I've had enough stress to last me a lifetime," she said as she started to leave. "All I want to do now is to have this baby and to settle down in peace to raise him.''

"Patrick is mine, too,'' Jeff retorted. "I can't let you walk out of my life now. Is this because of what my father said? If so, forget it. I'm out of here.''

"Partly, and because I just realized in some ways I've been no better than your father. I didn't really listen to what you kept telling me. I didn't realize how serious you were about wanting out of the hotel business. I thought you just didn't know what you wanted to do with your life. Now that I know you do, you have my blessings, but you'll have to go on without me.''

"Come on, Abby, you're just upset. Let me take you home. We can talk about this tomorrow when you feel better.''

"No. It wouldn't be fair to you to make you into the man I wanted you to be,'' Abby answered. "It's more that. We're still two different people. We look at life in different ways. I can't live that way again, and it's not fair for me to ask you to change for me. You'd only come to resent me for it,'' Abby answered, girding herself not to break down at the hurt look in Jeff's eyes.

"Give me a break, Abby,'' Jeff answered. His eyes conveyed his frustration; a white line formed around his tight lips. "I can handle Dad. As for my writing, I've been at it for a long time. My agent tells me he has someone who wants to look at my latest manuscript. So, as far as I can tell, this isn't about whether or not I work with my father or keep on writing—it's between you and me.''

''Perhaps,'' she answered. ''That's what I've been trying to tell you.''

''Please don't go like this, Abby,'' he said. ''Stay and talk to me. I'm sure we can work things out.''

''There's nothing left to talk about.'' She started to walk away, then turned back. ''I'll let you know when the baby is born.''

''JEFF? WHERE'S ABBY?''

''Gone.''

Elaine came to his side and took his hand in hers. ''If you love her, you shouldn't let her go.''

''Maybe it's for the best,'' he answered. ''She needed a little space.''

''Is that woman gone?'' Jeff's father growled.

Jeff was too heartbroken to do more than clench his fists and swallow his anger. No matter how angry his father made him, he was his father, after all. ''What do you mean by 'that woman'? She's gone for now, but Abby is the woman I hope to marry.''

''Ah—'' his father nodded knowingly ''—there's nothing wrong with marriage, but you picked a hell of a time to decide to become marriage-minded. And with a woman who's older than you. You can't possibly have known her for long. I knew from the minute I set eyes on her that she's the reason you can't make up your mind to go on the annual inspection tour with me!''

''Abby's being older than I am has nothing to do

with anything. She's more woman than any I've met. And she has nothing to do with my not wanting to go on the tour or not wanting to remain in the hotel business. In fact, she thinks I should.''

He strode to the window and looked down at the street where he could see Abby's cab pull away from the curb. ''I've been trying to tell you for some time that I'm not sure I want to join you in actively running the corporation. That I want to take the time to finish the book I'm working on.''

''Writing!'' His father snorted. ''A dreamer's game. From what I've heard, your chances of getting published are slim to none. And unless you're an exception, you'll never hit the jackpot anyway. I'm offering you something solid in the way of a future. So, now that this Abby Carson is gone, are you prepared to come with me?''

Jeff met his sister's gaze. She was the one person who could ultimately satisfy his father and get him off the hook. He raised an eyebrow in an unspoken question. She nodded.

''Only if you take Elaine with us, so that she can get some hands-on experience,'' Jeff replied. Elaine's brilliant smile told him he'd done the right thing.

With a last look out the window, he faced down his father. Even though a stubborn look came over the older man's face, Jeff went on. ''It's time for you to face facts, Dad. Of the two of us, Elaine is the one who belongs at your side, and, eventually, the one who should take over when you decide to retire. She's devoted herself to Logan hotels. She's worked with you behind the scenes for years. Too bad you haven't been able to see that the hotel business is in Elaine's blood."

As Abby is in mine, he thought.

ABBY LEANED BACK against the leather seat of the cab and wiped away the tears that gathered at the corners of her eyes. She saw Jeff's face in the face of every male passerby. And in each, she saw the pain in Jeff's eyes when she'd said goodbye.

She'd left because it had become time for her to take a good look at herself, her relationship with him and where it was taking her. The picture wasn't pretty.

If she expected Jeff to be more pragmatic and not to spend his life on a dream, maybe she, in turn, should try to become more of a risk-taker and a dreamer. Somehow, she should have compromised and enjoyed Jeff for the man he was and life as he saw it. But deep inside and no matter how much she'd come to love him, the conditioning of her past had left its mark. She needed stability and purpose...the way she defined it. She couldn't bring herself to tie her future into Jeff's.

So why did she feel her heart breaking into little pieces?

"JEFF, ARE YOU GOING to be okay?" Elaine's concerned question caught Jeff's attention.

"Yeah, except that these two weeks have been

the longest in my life." He'd reluctantly toured the Logan-owned or Logan-managed hotels with his father and his sister, but he'd packed away the ersatz diploma that Mrs. Anderson had lovingly written for him, and the books he'd bought to learn about fatherhood. But no matter which part of the country he was in, his thoughts were constantly on Abby.

"You're thinking about Abby, aren't you?"

"Truthfully, I am." He took a deep breath. There was no use trying to hide the obvious from his sister. "Abby's pregnant, and I'm the father."

"Oh, Jeff," Elaine said. She threw her arms around him and hugged him. "I'm so sorry."

"I'm not," he answered. "It's just that I keep wondering how she's getting along. According to the books I've read, she must be beginning to show. I keep wondering what her family must think of me now that I'm out of the picture."

He smiled sadly, and added wistfully, "We named him Patrick. Wouldn't it be a kick if he turned out to be a Patricia."

Tears came into Elaine's eyes. "You can still be his father."

"Yeah, sure. I promised myself and Abby to be the best dad a kid could have. I even took a crash course on kids and read a ton of books to get ready. Instead, it looks as if I'm only going to be a part-time father. That is, if I'm lucky."

"If you love her so much, why don't you go after her? Surely enough time has passed for both of you to know if you want each other."

"I love Abby more than ever," he replied. "But I promised myself I'd give her space, and that's what I have to do."

Since he'd returned, he mused wistfully, he'd wandered down to the hotel's child care center. The children had been happy to see him. He'd been happy to see them, too. Not that he'd stayed very long. The memories of the surprisingly happy hours spent there were too deep, too hurtful. He missed Mike, and Wally, too. And the look of compassion on Mrs. Anderson's face when she'd inquired about Abby had been more than he could bear.

In the last two weeks, every time he'd encountered a family, a mother, father and a baby, he saw himself, Abby and a little fair-haired, green-eyed boy named Patrick. And each time, his heart had ached for what could have been.

Chapter Twelve

"What have you done to my mother?"

At the sound of the accusing voice, Jeff turned back at the door to his office. "Kate?"

"Mom's pregnant!" she blurted. "And it's all your fault!"

"Come on inside," Jeff said, hoping for a more private conversation. "It looks as if we need to have a heart-to-heart."

"Is Abby okay?" he asked once they were inside.

"Sort of," Kate answered angrily. "But she's not herself. How could you do that to her?"

"I loved Abby, that's all. As a matter of fact," he went on now that his heartbeat had slowed to normal, "I still do. I didn't walk away. You might say, I was pushed. As for the baby, Patrick, he might not have been planned, but I'm not sorry about him. And as far as I know, neither is your mother."

"Grandma told me Mom cries herself to sleep every night! If you love her like you say you do, how come Mom says she hasn't seen or spoken to you in weeks?"

Jeff felt terrible about Kate's struggle to contain herself, but he wasn't sure how much of the story he ought to tell her. "I think your mother should be the one to tell you," Jeff answered. "Have you asked her?"

"I've known for a long time that there was something between the two of you," Kate answered. "I even thought it was cool for Mom to finally fall in love again. But she won't talk about what's wrong now, so I decided to come here to talk to you."

Kate looked so upset as she followed him into his office. Maybe it was just as well that he wasn't her stepfather, he thought wryly. All he seemed to be able to do since he met Abby was make her and her family unhappy. On the other hand, it was a title he still hoped to acquire some day....

"How's Sebastian?" he asked as he waved her to a chair and walked around his desk to his own.

"He's fine," she answered firmly, "but don't change the subject. I want to know why you and my mother aren't speaking to each other. You say you love her, and Grandma says Mom loves you. How can two people love each other and still not be able to talk to each other?"

"Good question," Jeff said thoughtfully. Maybe he should have waited a few days and then insisted that he and Abby meet to talk things over instead of waiting this long. "Pride, I guess. And then I had to leave town on business. I've just gotten back."

"So what are you going to do about Mom?"

"I've been thinking about it," Jeff answered. "I just haven't been able to decide—"

"If you really loved each other—and you say you do—that's all that matters. That's the way I felt about Sebastian when everyone thought he was too old for me. We're very happy, especially now that I'm pregnant. So, why don't you call Mom and tell her you love her and want to make up?"

"I'm not so sure Abby wants to listen." He sighed and studied Kate. Even through her frustration, he could see that she was happy in her marriage. And now she was starting a family. Jeff could imagine how happy Sebastian was. He wondered how Abby felt, becoming a mother and grandmother at the same time. Kate deserved a lot of credit for her courage in coming to see him.

"You're looking well, Kate. Marriage must agree with you."

"It's the babies," she answered with a happy smile, her attention diverted.

"Babies?"

"Twins," she grinned. "Sebastian is beside himself. So am I. I've wanted to be a mother ever since I was thirteen years old."

"Congratulations. It must be a blast being pregnant at the same time as your mother." He grinned. "You can compare notes, maybe even do exercises together. And if Sebastian needs any pointers on fatherhood, I have a few books on the subject I can give him. There's even a school I can recommend for practice on being a father."

"It would be a bigger blast if you were my step-father," she answered wistfully. "Then Mom would be happy, too."

Kate was a grown woman with a child of her own on the way, and still she was worrying about her mother, Jeff thought fondly as he listened to her lecture. In fact, he realized he *felt* like her stepfather. "Are you on a special diet, or would you like to come with me to the coffee shop for chocolate chip cookies and milk?"

"Cookies? What do cookies have to do with anything?"

Jeff didn't blame Kate for looking confused. His invitation had come out of left field. "Well, to tell the truth, I discovered a long time ago that chocolate chip cookies are the best kind of comfort food there is." He smiled ruefully. "Maybe if I'd insisted on giving Abby the cookie I made for her, we would have been married by now."

"Sounds confusing, but if you feel that way, what's keeping you from bringing Mom the cookie now?"

Jeff thought about it. Why *not* now? Only someone as young and pragmatic as Kate could have cut through to the obvious answer. He, the supposed risk-taker, couldn't see the forest for the trees.

ARMED WITH AN ODD-SHAPED goody bag tied with a yellow ribbon, Jeff rang for admittance to Abby's building.

"Yes?"

The voice was Caroline's. Damn! He'd hoped to find Abby alone. He took a deep breath. There was no turning back now.

"It's Jeff, Caroline. Is Abby at home? I wanted to talk with her."

"She's taking a nap," Abby's mother answered. "Besides, I'm not sure she wants to see you."

"Abby may not know it, but she does want to see me," he coaxed. "How about letting me in, and we'll both find out."

"Maybe I shouldn't," Caroline finally answered, "but I will. This has gone on long enough." The buzzer sounded. "Come on up."

A few minutes later, she held the door open for Jeff. "What's in the bag?"

"My version of a peace pipe."

"That doesn't make a bit of sense, young man, but come on in. I'll go and see if Abby is awake."

"How about letting me see if Abby is awake?" Jeff answered.

"One question first," Caroline said, blocking the way inside the apartment. "Is it true that you're the father of the baby Abby's expecting?"

"Cross my heart and hope to die," he said. He would have suited action to words, but the goody bag got in the way. "And I hope to become Abby's husband in the near future."

"It's about time. That's what we need—another wedding to liven up the place." Caroline eyed him sternly. "But I expect you to do something to put a smile back on Abby's face now." She waved at the door to Abby's bedroom, then headed for the kitchen.

Jeff tapped on the bedroom door. When there was no answer, he slowly opened the door and walked in. Abby was fast asleep on her back, one arm folded protectively across her stomach. From where he stood, he could see the obvious bulge that was Patrick.

He tiptoed to the bed, sat down at the edge, and gazed at Abby's tear-streaked cheeks. Calling himself stupid for waiting this long to come to her, he gently touched her face. He needed to see if she was real, and not just another dream in the chain of unhappy dreams he'd had almost nightly since she'd walked out of his life. Longingly, lovingly, he gently brushed the few strands of golden hair that had fallen across her forehead.

Abby's eyes opened slowly. She awakened with a start.

"Jeff?"

"Yes," he answered. "No, don't get up," he said when she started to pull herself up. "Just give me a few minutes. I need to tell you something. Okay?"

Her troubled eyes widened. She hesitantly nodded.

"Someone we both know made me realize I was stupidly suffering from a large dose of pride, and I decided she was right. I should have come sooner, but I'm here now. I just wanted to talk to you for a few minutes, to see if you and the baby are okay."

She lay back against the pillows. "We're fine. How did you get in? How have you been?"

"In answer to question number one—Caroline let me in," he answered. "As for question number two—not too good. But I have high hopes things are going to improve. As a matter of fact, to help things along, I brought some comfort food for you."

Abby felt as if she was living a dream. The twinkle in Jeff's eyes told one story. But the dark circles under his eyes told another. Their separation couldn't have been easy for him, either.

"What kind of comfort food did—?"

The twinkle faded from Jeff's eyes when she suddenly gasped.

"Something wrong?"

"No. Something is very right." She held her hand on her belly and smiled. "Patrick kicked me. I guess he overheard the bit about comfort food."

"In that case, maybe you *had* better get up so you can eat it," Jeff replied. "Here, let me help you."

Abby came into Jeff's arms with a grateful sigh. It felt so good, so natural, so wonderful to be held in his arms again. The memory of the interminable, empty days since she'd walked away from him slowly began to fade.

How could she have left him? How could she have let her pride prevent her from going back and telling him that she loved him just as he was, and that she didn't care if he never changed from the man he was? That she loved the zany way he'd tried to learn about fatherhood? That she didn't care if he wanted to hole up and write mystery stories. That it was fine with her if he changed his mind and worked with his father.

Nothing mattered as long as they were together.

"Sit down, Abby," he said when they were in the kitchen. He handed her the goody bag.

Abby untied the yellow ribbon and peered into the bag. "A cookie? You're sure cookies are comfort food?"

"As sure as thirty years of experience can make me," he answered. He drew a single heart-shaped cookie out of the bag. "I had Wolfgang bake it especially for you and keep it in a freezer for me. I think I knew all along we'd get together again."

Abby's happy tears flowed down her cheeks.

"Don't cry, Abby," he said, coming to her side and taking her in his arms. He kissed the salty tears away from her cheeks. "I only wanted to see you smile. I only want to make you happy."

"I am," she answered in a shaken voice. "I truly am, but I can't seem to turn off the spigot."

"I may have a remedy for that," he said into her lips. "Will you marry me, Abby?"

Against his lips, Abby said, "Yes."

Against his waist, Patrick kicked his approval.

Jeff swallowed hard.

"My father and Elaine will be in town for the weekend," he said. "How about I pick you up and we all have dinner at the hotel?"

"Do they know about Patrick?"

"Only Elaine does." Jeff smiled. "My sister doesn't miss a thing. She told me she sensed we loved each other. She even told me she'd guessed about Patrick even before I told her. She said you had a certain look in your eyes that gave you away. In fact, Elaine wanted me to come after you that very morning and ask you to marry me."

"I wish you had," Abby answered. "But you're here now—that's all that counts."

Jeff kissed her with all the pent-up longings inside him. The way Abby returned his embrace told him that she'd missed him, too. "Yes, sweetheart, I'm here now," he said. "And I'm never going to let you go again."

They stood there, holding each other close, until Abby reached for the cookie and broke it in two. They stood there, eating the cookie and grinning foolishly at each other.

"I've never eaten anything so good," she said.

"Thank you," Jeff answered modestly. "I might even decide to take up baking cookies as a career later on."

"Somehow, I don't think so," Abby answered. "But if you do…"

"Abby," Jeff said, hugging her close. "What am I going to do with you!"

"Love me," she whispered. "Just love me."

It was moments before Jeff came to his senses. "So, what about dinner? Elaine says she thinks Dad wants to apologize to you properly."

"As long as the three of you are already there,

there's no point in coming all the way here to pick me up,'' Abby said. ''I'll take a cab and meet you there.''

''You're sure?''

''I'm sure.''

''Promise?'' Jeff kissed the tip of Abby's nose.

''Promise.''

BUZZED INTO THE PRIVATE elevator that took her to the Logan Wilshire owner's penthouse suite, Abby found Jeff's father waiting for her. He was smiling, but she sensed hostility behind that smile. If the man was regretful, it wasn't obvious. Instinct told her that his genial demeanor was a sham.

If Jeff hadn't assured her that his father was anxious to meet her and apologize, she would have turned on her heel and left.

''Good evening, Ms. Carson,'' he said, holding open the door to the suite. ''Come right in. Jeff's been called away on business, but he'll be back shortly.''

Patrick began to kick; Abby's stomach started to churn. From experience, Abby realized both reactions spelled bad news.

Before he could continue, Jeff's sister Elaine came to meet her. Dressed in a short brown chiffon cocktail dress that was accented by the trademark Logan golden-brown hair and brandy-colored eyes, her smile seemed to be genuine enough. Even so, Abby couldn't shake her growing sense of apprehension.

Elaine smiled and shook Abby's outstretched hand.

"I'm so glad we're going to have the opportunity to get to know you, Abby. Jeff has told me so many wonderful things about you."

"Thank you." Expecting to see Jeff's mother, Abby looked around the room. "Is your mother here tonight?"

"No, I'm afraid not. She's off representing the corporation at a public relations conference in London. I'm sure she'll want to meet you when she gets back."

"She's only there because I can't be in several places at one time." Jeff's father grunted. "I asked Jeff to attend, but he said he had urgent business here." He shot Abby a sour look and strode to the bar. "Drink, Ms. Carson?" he called over his shoulder.

"Just a ginger ale, thank you," Abby replied, her nerve endings on alert. "Please call me Abby."

He shrugged. "Of course, and please call me Addams. I use my middle name so that no one will mistake me for Jeff."

Abby smiled faintly. Where Jeff was tall and lithe, his father was shorter and verging on paunchy. Where his father frowned, Jeff smiled. As far as Abby could see, the only thing Addams Logan had in common with his son *was* the name.

"I take it you don't drink?" he asked as he poured a can of ginger ale into a frosted glass. Even that innocuous question put Abby on her guard. She sensed that she was going to have to pay more attention to what she said, or the man would be all over her like chewing gum.

"No. Not anymore," Abby replied. She bit her lip at the speculation that sprang into the man's eyes as his gaze swung to her middle. The flowing trapeze gown that she wore was concealing, but she was sure the man wasn't that unaware of her condition.

"Why don't you come and sit down beside me, Abby?" Elaine invited her with a warning glance at her father. She patted the cushion beside her. "Jeff should be back in a moment or two."

If their meeting tonight was meant to be a fresh start, what did Elaine's expression mean? Abby wondered uneasily. The answer that shot into her mind was enough to make Patrick become more excited than ever. In spite of Addams's attempt to smile, the man didn't care for her, or at least what she represented.

Addams Logan waited until Abby sat down on the couch and handed her her drink. He'd added a twist of lime and a sprig of mint to make it look festive, but nothing in his attitude indicated tonight was an occasion for celebration.

"I'm not the type to beat around the bush, Abby," he stated, remaining standing and looking down at her. "Jeff told me the two of you plan on getting married soon."

To Abby, the statement sounded more like an accusation than a question. She took a deep breath. Forewarned was forearmed.

"Yes," she replied, her sixth sense clamoring. From the tight sound in the man's voice, she sensed that this wasn't going to be a polite let's-get-acquainted conversation. "When did you say Jeff would be back?"

Elaine looked at her father reproachfully and put a reassuring hand on Abby's knee. "I'm sure he'll be back any minute. Tell me, when are you and Jeff planning on getting married?"

"As soon as we can make arrangements," Abby answered. She felt as though she was on trial. She glanced at her watch—surely, Jeff should be back by now.

"Elaine mentioned that you have a grown daughter, Ms—Abby." Jeff's father corrected himself with a weak smile and went on. "How old would she be?"

Since Abby figured the man was bound to find out the facts of her life sooner or later, she answered, "Kate is twenty-one, and newly married."

The feeling that there was an ulterior motive behind the questions grew stronger. Whatever game the man was playing, she didn't want to play any part in it.

Watching the expressions cross his face, Abby suspected Addams Logan was a single-minded man. Maybe that was why he was such a success in business. But as far as she was concerned, he was a bust as a father. She set her unfinished drink on the coffee table and started to rise.

"I hope you're not leaving," he said with a cool smile that barely lifted his lips. "We've only just begun to get acquainted. Haven't we, Elaine?"

Elaine nodded slowly. She gave Abby a sympathetic look as if she understood Abby's reaction. "You *are* going to be a member of our family, Abby. I suppose it's only natural for my father to want to know more about you."

Maybe she had been wrong, Abby thought. At least, Elaine looked friendly enough. But from Addams's set lips, Abby knew she didn't meet with the man's approval.

"That would put you at about...let me guess," he went on. "A good ten years older than my son?"

Abby's heart sank. Beside her, she heard Elaine catch her breath. Abby wanted to leave before the questions became more and more personal. She gazed around the suite, as cold and devoid of charm as was Jeff's father. A pity, when Jeff and his sister were so warm and friendly.

Determined not to make whatever the man had in mind easier for him, Abby stood up. "What difference does that make?"

Patrick kicked again. Poor little boy, Abby thought, gazing into Addams's cold eyes. It was going to be difficult for him to ever please his stiff-necked grandfather. For grandfather he certainly was—whether or not she and Jeff married.

"Ah, but how will Jeff eventually feel about your

having a daughter only a few years younger than himself? Forgive me for being so blunt," he went on without waiting for an answer, "but someone has to say this. Someone has to be sensible."

Abby froze.

"Ten years from now," he went on, "the question will be, is my son going to be satisfied with a fifty-year-old woman? After all, Jeff will be young enough, and if he stays with the Logan Corporation, wealthy enough to be attractive to a younger woman. I've even said as much to Jeff."

Upset at hearing her own lingering fears voiced, Abby made up her mind. Jeff or no Jeff, she had to leave.

Her eyes locked with his. "That's a question only your son can answer. And forgive *me* for being so blunt, but I don't see what my age has to do with our 'getting acquainted.'"

"A lot. And one more thing," Jeff's father added with deadly calm. "You should know that if Jeff marries you, I will disinherit him."

"Dad! How can you talk to Abby that way?" Elaine exclaimed, rushing to Abby's side. "You promised me you'd be civil, that you would apologize. That you would at least try to get to know her before you formed an opinion."

With a determined look, her father waved her away.

Abby had had enough. More than enough. "I'm sorry for you, Mr. Logan, and all that you're going to miss. If you feel you have to disinherit your son if he marries me, by all means do it. That's between the two of you. But worst of all, you're going to lose a grandchild in the bargain.'' She turned to Elaine. ''Please tell Jeff I've gone home.''

Apparently satisfied, Jeff's father finally smiled, a genuinely pleased smile. ''I was sure you'd understand. You're a mature woman. And as Jeff's father, I'm only interested in his welfare.''

Abby wanted to tell him that the only thing he was interested in was trying to mold Jeff and any future Logan in his own image.

As far as she could see, Jeff's happiness was the least of his father's concerns. But Jeff was a grown man; she couldn't fight his battles for him. And the way her stomach was churning, she wasn't prepared to try. She headed for the door.

''By the way, Ms. Carson,'' Addams Logan called after her. ''The baby that you're carrying, whose ever it is. Send me your doctor bills and I'll take care of them.''

Abby saw red. ''This is your own grandchild!'' She didn't wait to hear the reply. She headed out the door, intending never to look back.

Instead, as the elevator doors opened, she ran straight into Jeff.

Chapter Thirteen

Jeff caught Abby in his arms. "I'm sorry I got held up downstairs. Thank goodness, it turned out to be a false alarm." When she didn't say anything, he held her away from him. "Why are you looking like that? What's the matter? Where are you going?"

Abby shook her head, too upset to talk. Blinded with tears, she held back a sob, ran into the elevator and stabbed at the "down" button. Before Jeff could react, the doors closed and Abby disappeared.

Too stunned to move, Jeff stared at the closed elevator door, then at the door to his suite. Abby hadn't closed it behind her.

Cold chills ran through him as he realized something was terribly wrong. And just who was the cause of it.

Abby had been right, he thought as he made up his mind to end this farce. He wasn't a child to be ordered around. He was old enough to make his own choices, to make up his mind what he wanted out of life and go for it. He could either cave in and keep his father happy, or finally get off the Logan merry-go-round and marry Abby. Gazing at the blank mahogany elevator door, Jeff realized he'd come too far to turn back. He couldn't have it both ways. There was no in-between. Not any longer. He grit his teeth and strode through the door to the suite.

"What did you say to Abby?" he demanded, confronting his father. "What did you do to make her leave like that?"

"Nothing I shouldn't have," his father answered. "I only tried to make her face the fact she's older than you are. And that this affair of yours is probably nothing more than a passing infatuation on your part."

Jeff couldn't believe what he was hearing. He turned to his sister. "Elaine?"

"I tried to stop Dad," she told Jeff, "but it was no use. He thinks he's doing the right thing for you."

"Like hell, he does," Jeff answered, struggling to control his temper. "I'll bet that's not all he said to Abby, or she wouldn't have been so upset."

"Well, I guess there was a little more than that."

"A hell of a lot more, unless I miss my guess. As a matter of fact, I wouldn't put it past him to have arranged for me to be called downstairs on a wild goose chase to get me out of the way." His father's flushed face told Jeff that he was right.

"What else did you say to Abby?" Jeff demanded.

"Only that I would disinherit you if you married her. Of course, before she left," he added magnanimously, "I offered to pay all of the expenses for the baby she's expecting."

Father or no, Jeff wanted to strike out blindly. He clenched his fists. "How could you have hurt Abby like that? Didn't you get the message that I love her? I intend to marry her if she's still willing to have me after you've gotten through with her!"

"Willing to marry you, my eye," his father sputtered. "Hell, the woman looks as if she's smart enough to know a good thing when she sees one. You're young and the heir to a fortune in real estate! She couldn't find a better catch than you."

"She's not that shallow. In fact, I had to convince her to marry me."

"Good God, Jeffrey. I did you a favor! I thought you'd gotten over that fool nonsense about marrying that woman by now!"

"Don't call Abby 'that woman' again!" Jeff bit out. "And if you thought I'd get over loving her, you thought wrong," he added, turning on his heel. "I'm going to go after Abby, apologize for your behavior, and beg her to marry me—if she'll still have me. And one more thing," he added, bracing himself for an argument, "I've decided I'm not cut out for the corporate life. I intend to make a success of my writing. No, don't answer," Jeff said when his father started to shout at him. "You have Elaine. She's a far better choice of a successor than I am."

HER EYES STILL BLINDED by tears, Abby gratefully made her way into her apartment. The first person she saw was her ex-husband.

"Richard! I'm so glad you're here!" Sobbing, Abby fell into his arms.

Richard caught her and held her close. Stroking her hair, he murmured his reassurance and led her to the couch. The remains of Chinese takeout were on the coffee table.

"Kate called me a few days ago. She told me she was worried about you. I couldn't leave for Los Angeles right away, but I got here as soon as I could. Whatever it is that's bothering you, maybe I can help."

Abby hiccuped to a stop. "Bless you," she said. "You're just the man I need to talk to right now."

"Having trouble with Jeff?" Smiling, Richard brushed away the tears that lingered on her cheeks.

"Not exactly. My problem is with his father. He made me so angry when he insinuated I wanted to marry Jeff for his money, I wanted to hit him." She took the handkerchief that Richard handed her and wiped her eyes.

"Maybe the man is afraid of losing his son. Some parents are, you know."

"I doubt it—not from the way he speaks to Jeff. I'm afraid it's more than that. It's me. He doesn't believe I love Jeff."

"Any man would be a fool not to realize what a wonderful woman you are, Abby. It didn't take a fortune-teller with a crystal ball to see that the two of you were in love when I was here for Kate's wedding. So, what happened? Has Jeff changed his mind about wanting to get married?''

"No, he wasn't even there.'' She wrapped her arms around herself for comfort. She went on to tell him all the things Jeff's father had said. "The only thing he said that made sense was that I was older than Jeff. He even threatened to disinherit Jeff if he married me. Then he suggested the baby I'm carrying possibly wasn't Jeff's! I had to leave before I hit him.''

"Attagirl.'' Richard smiled his approval. "But don't you think you should have waited for Jeff to show up before you walked out?''

"I couldn't.'' Her tears started up again. "Not when I was ready to murder his father.''

"Now that doesn't sound a bit like you. Why don't you tell me all about everything, including the baby,'' Richard coaxed. "We are good friends, aren't we?''

"The best.''

"Then let's talk. Maybe there's some way I can help you.''

He put a pillow behind Abby's back, lifted her feet to the coffee table, and put his arm around her. "Here you go.''

With a sigh, Abby cuddled into his welcome warmth. "You'll never know how grateful I am to find you here,'' she told him.

"Any time,'' he answered with a light laugh. "All you have to do is ask. That's what friends are for. How did you get yourself into this mess, anyway?''

Gazing up into his smile, Abby realized Jeff had been right. Richard was still in love with her.

The problem was that she loved someone else.

''You're not going to believe me when I tell you everything started when I read my horoscope in the newspaper on my way to Acapulco.''

''Kate told me you'd disappeared earlier this year. But you're right,'' Richard answered, ''I can hardly believe it. That's not the way you operate.''

''Maybe not. I guess I've changed more than I know. Anyway, my horoscope featured a romantic interlude. It even asked if I was ready for love and marriage and said, if I was, that a Cancer native would play an exciting role in my life. I couldn't get the question out of my mind. It was as if someone or something was offering me a last chance to change my life. By the time the plane landed, I was ready.''

''That doesn't sound like you, either.'' Richard laughed. ''*I've* always been the romantic dreamer who believed in off-the-wall things like horoscopes. You've always been the pragmatic one. Especially when we were married.''

''In retrospect, I know it sounds strange,'' Abby agreed, ''but that horoscope began to change me. And when I met Jeff, I was captivated with him. Maybe because it was my birthday. I wanted to have an adventure before it was too late.''

''All you had to do was call on me, Abby. My

whole life has been a series of adventures. I would have been willing to share one with you. But that was what you took exception to about me, remember?''

''I remember,'' Abby answered thoughtfully. ''But there was Kate to think of back then. Children need stability, and I was so sure you'd never change. That's what made what happened in Acapulco so unexpected. I was the one who changed—but obviously not enough.''

''Well, you were probably right about me back then. But if you had been capable of seeing life as an adventure at the time, we'd probably still be married.''

''Maybe, but even after the horoscope came true and I met Jeff, when I got back home I turned back into the same old predictable, security-conscious Abby I was before,'' Abby said bitterly. She couldn't tell him about the name she'd used in Mexico. The joke about Scarlett O'Malley was too precious to share—even with Richard. ''Instead of appreciating Jeff for the man he was, I tried to change him.''

''I gather things haven't worked the way you wanted?''

''No. It couldn't. He was trying to please both his father and me at the same time. In ways you can't begin to imagine,'' Abby answered, thinking of Jeff's stint at the child care center. ''I wanted him to be more pragmatic, more decisive, no matter which career he chose for himself. It wasn't for financial security for me. I wanted him to become a man who could count on himself, who'd be there for me and the baby. I was afraid he'd keep changing his mind, go from one idea to another. I finally realized it wasn't fair to ask him to try to change from the man he was into the man I wanted him to be."

"But you fell in love with the man he was, didn't you?"

"Yes."

"So why try to change him?"

"I was wrong. I should have forgotten the past and lived for the present and the future."

"Is that why you were crying?"

"No. We got together again. Actually, I was crying because I was so angry at Jeff's father. As for Jeff, I know I still love him. But that's no excuse to try to change him. Or to expect him to make a career decision for me. Any more than I had any excuses to try to change you years ago. No wonder you agreed to a divorce."

"Don't worry about it now, Abby," Richard assured her with a lingering smile. "I did okay. So has Kate. Besides, we've been good friends all these years, haven't we?"

Abby brushed her middle. "More than friends. I suppose you might say that, in a way, we've never stopped loving each other. But now there's a baby to think of."

"Are you sorry about the baby?"

"Funny the way people keep asking me that. No,

actually I'm very happy. It's just that the way things have been going, the baby might not have a live-in father.''

There was a pause. ''Don't worry about that, Abby. I promise you, one way or another, the baby will have a father.''

''The baby is about the only thing that *is* right with me,'' Abby went on. She turned in his arms. ''Kate didn't tell you about the baby before?''

''No, but I guessed.'' He grinned. ''The kid is too loyal to give away your secrets. And I never asked.'' He set Abby aside and rose. ''Hungry? There's some extra Chinese in the kitchen that I can microwave for you.''

''No, thanks.'' Abby groaned and rubbed her stomach. ''Not with the way I feel.''

''In that case, maybe I'd better get this stuff out from under your nose. No need to upset you any more than you already are. And by the way, I have a solution to your problem.''

''I don't see how,'' Abby answered. ''Things are so bad, they couldn't possibly get better.''

''Sure they can,'' Richard answered. ''You could marry me again. I wouldn't mind being a father to your Patrick. In fact, it would fun.''

Abby broke out in tears.

''Hey, I didn't mean to upset you! You don't have to make up your mind right away. I'll put this stuff in the kitchen and we'll talk.''

When he came back, Richard took a deep breath and looked down at Abby. She'd fallen asleep. He covered her with an afghan, turned down the lights and went off to do something for Abby that he never would have done if he hadn't loved her so much.

RICHARD COLLIDED WITH Jeff just as he came through the door to the building. He caught Jeff by the arm. "Hold up a minute, Logan. I need to talk to you."

Jeff glared at him. Tangling with Abby's ex was the last thing he wanted. What he did want was to find Abby and tell her of his decision to leave the Logan hotel chain. And more importantly, how much he loved her. "Make it later, why don't you? I've had enough of finding you around here. Right now, I'm looking for Abby."

"That's what I wanted to talk to you about," Richard answered ruefully. "Come on inside the lobby. I think you'll be interested in what I have to say."

"I doubt it," Jeff grumbled. "But go ahead. Just don't take too long."

"It's about Abby," Richard said, staring into Jeff's narrowed eyes. "Now, don't go off the deep end. It's not what you think."

"Are you trying to tell me Abby doesn't want to see me? If so, I'm going to have to hear her say it."

"No. As a matter of fact, when Abby told me about the baby, I asked her to marry me again so the baby would have a father."

"That's it!" Jeff exclaimed, infuriated. "Where

do you get off thinking you're going to use that excuse to get Abby back?''

"Hey, wait a minute," Richard said, raising his hands to fend off Jeff. "I was only trying to help Abby. She turned me down."

"Damn right, she did." Jeff took a deep breath to calm down. "Get this straight! I'm not letting anyone be a father to my child but me!"

"Then go upstairs and tell that to Abby," Richard answered. "But let me tell you, I'm no classic hero. I'm not doing this for you. I'm doing this for Abby."

Jeff looked Richard in the eye. What he saw there made him realize that Richard loved his ex-wife enough to give her up. He was a far better man than Jeff had thought him to be.

Jeff reached out his hand, took Richard's into his and shook it fervently. "Truce. And my sincere apologies for being a jerk."

"NOT AGAIN!" Caroline blocked the door. "You can't come in. I don't want Abby any more upset than she already is."

"Me, neither," Jeff assured her. "If you let me inside, I promise you that what I have to tell her will make Abby happy."

He put his heart and soul into a smile that he hoped would pave the way back past Caroline. "What do you say? May I come in?"

"For Abby," her mother said sternly. "She's

asleep on the couch. But I'll be in my room, just in case." She softened her words with a wink.

Jeff made his way to the couch where Abby lay sleeping. He could see the path her tears had taken down her cheeks. Could see her lips move as she said something in her sleep.

His heart near to breaking, he knelt beside the couch, took one of her hands in his, and gently kissed the tips of each finger. How could anyone hurt such a gentle, loving person as Abby?

He had to admit that he'd done his share by not going after Abby as soon as he'd heard what his father had said to her. He'd wanted to give her space—to think, to make sure she still wanted to marry him after all the awful things his father must have said about him.

Wrong! He'd learned his lesson. He didn't intend to waste another precious moment of his love for Abby.

"Abby, love," he whispered into her ear. "I'm here. Wake up."

Abby stirred, murmured something under her breath and fell back to sleep again.

Jeff laughed softly. Cuddled into the patchwork afghan, Abby looked like an innocent young girl waiting for her prince to rescue her.

And rescue her, he would. She'd once called him her knight in shining armor. Tonight, he intended to be all of that—and more.

"Abby, love," he repeated. "Wake up. We have a plane to catch."

Her expressive eyes opened slowly, as if she couldn't believe what she heard and saw. "Jeff?"

"In the flesh, sweetheart." He bent and gently kissed her forehead, her cheeks, her lips.

"How did you get here?"

"Kate and Richard sent me," he said with a smile. "No," he added, getting to his feet and joining her on the edge of the couch, "that's not exactly true. My love for you brought me here. And this time, nothing will stop me from marrying you."

"Not even your father's wishes?"

"Not even that. I've made up my mind about Dad. I respect him as my father, but I intend to live my life the way I want to."

Jeff punctuated his sentences with kisses, each one bringing him closer to Abby. He tossed away the afghan to get closer. Soon, she was in his arms, his length stretched alongside hers. They lay so close that they were almost one. He bent over her, kissed her again and whispered his heart's yearnings.

"I love you, Abby, more than words can say. To me, you're the earth, the moon, the stars—the universe rolled into one. Please say you'll marry me. I want nothing more than for you and Patrick to belong to me."

He waited only a split second before he went on. "I'll buy that house in Westwood that we both love so much. I always wanted a tree house when I was a kid, but we always lived in hotels. I'll build a tree house for Patrick to play in. We can invite Kate's babies over to play with him. We can turn the whole backyard into a playground, if that's what you want. I'll—''

Near tears again, Abby laughed shakingly and hugged Jeff close. She kissed his lips, the small cleft in his chin, the throbbing vein in his neck. ''Enough! Of course, I'll marry you. In fact, I think I've belonged to you from the moment I met you under a new moon in Acapulco.''

''Thank you.'' Jeff hugged her and sighed with relief. ''We'll get married and honeymoon at the Concordia.'' He pulled himself away reluctantly. ''It's too late to go anywhere tonight. As much as I'd like to stay here with you, I have to go back to the hotel, clear up some loose ends, and change our plane tickets. Why don't you get a good rest? I hate to leave you, but I'll come for you tomorrow morning and we can pick up where we left off.''

''Promise?''

''I promise.''

JUST AS ABBY FINISHED her packing the next morning, the telephone rang.

''Abby, I hate to have to tell you this,'' said Jeff, ''but Elaine just called and told me Dad had a light stroke. Elaine and Mom are with him, and they want me to come up to San Francisco right away.''

''Of course,'' Abby answered. She was disappointed, but a father was a father, after all. ''Go ahead. I'll wait for you.''

''Better not. I don't know how long I'll be.

Maybe you'd better go on. You could use some rest and relaxation before we get married. I have a car waiting to take me to the airport. I'll join you as soon as I can.''

Weddings were hard to plan—honeymoons sometimes even harder, Abby thought as she put down the telephone. Her luggage was packed, the airline tickets to Acapulco Jeff had sent over by messenger were in her purse. She might as well take his advice and meet him there. Besides, her mother had decided to go away for the weekend, and she didn't relish spending the time alone in an empty apartment.

Would Jeff's father always manage to come between them? she wondered. Nonsense, she told herself. The man was ill, had probably worked himself into a stroke over Jeff's announcement that he was getting married this weekend.

She couldn't insist that Jeff come with her now. Not when his father was so ill. She remembered Jeff had told her that he wanted a large family. The last thing she wanted was to have him walk away from his father or break his family ties. She'd take his advice and wait for him at the Concordia Hotel.

The new Abby took over. Regardless of his reasons for not joining her—and they certainly were good ones—she intended to make him pay for making her wait for her wedding day. Smiling to herself, she called for a cab.

THE DESK CLERK at the Concordia Hotel in Acapulco shook his head. "I'm sorry, Señor. There is no Ms. Carson registered at the hotel. Are you sure you have the right name?"

"Maybe you remember her. She's a petite blonde with sea-green eyes. And a smile that breaks your heart. Oh, and she's expecting a baby."

The clerk raised his eyebrows. How often did a man seek a pregnant woman whose name he didn't know?

"How about a Scarlett O'Malley?"

"Ah, yes," the clerk replied, checking his computer. "But I'm afraid I cannot give you her room number without permission. Did you want me to call?"

"No, thanks," Jeff answered. Two could play the game Abby had started. And for a man raised in the hotel industry, finding Abby would be no problem. No problem at all.

In her room, Abby had undressed and, clad only in a light robe, opened the doors of the patio. She stood on the balcony and looked out over the hotel gardens to the distant beach where the warm waters of the bay lapped against the shore. The sun was setting with a burst of colors: red, orange, yellow. Below her, a riot of hibiscus bushes looked as if an artist had painted them there.

Exhausted by a day of wandering along the beach, Abby took a shower, put on the robe and lay down on the bed to rest.

The road back to Acapulco and Jeff hadn't been easy. But in retrospect, it was worth it. She and Jeff had both changed to be able to reach this point.

She'd found in herself a woman she liked much better than the old, staid Abby Carson. And in doing so, had found the man of her dreams.

It seemed as if only minutes had passed when she heard a knock on the door. Thinking it was room service delivering the light meal she'd ordered earlier, Abby opened the door.

Jeff stood there, a broad smile on his face, a flaming red mass of hibiscus flowers in one hand and a wedding ring in the other. The love that shone from his twinkling eyes filled her empty heart.

"Scarlett O'Malley, I believe?"

Abby nodded; tears of happiness filled her eyes.

"Are you ready to marry me and let me be a father to Patrick?" he asked solemnly. "Will you let me try to make all your dreams come true?"

"I can't think of anything I would like more," Abby answered, throwing the door wide open. "But first, I have a question."

"Ask me anything, sweetheart. I'm all yours."

Abby smiled through tears of happiness. "What's your astrological sign?"

"My astrological sign?" He thought for a moment. "Cancer. I was born in July. Why?"

"I thought so," she answered, drawing him into the room. The forecast she'd read on the plane had come true. He was the most exciting and romantic man she'd ever met, and the possibilities of a full and rewarding life with him were endless.

Jeff put the flowers on a coffee table, took Abby's left hand and slid the wedding ring on her finger.

"I've made arrangements for us to get married in the morning, Abby, but do you mind if we have the honeymoon first?"

Abby dropped the robe from her shoulders. "I don't mind a bit."

Epilogue

"Mr. Logan! Mr. Logan!" The desk nurse in the maternity ward rushed into the scrub room. "I have an important message for you!"

"Tell me later," Jeff replied, tying on the green hospital robe. "I don't have time for messages. I'm going to have a baby!"

The nurse burst into laughter. "That would be a first around here. I don't think any of us could take it."

Jeff paused as he scrubbed his hands with rough hospital soap. "Heck." He grinned. "I meant my wife is having a baby."

"Sure," she answered. "And she's probably doing fine. It's the fathers we worry about around here." For a minute, she gazed at Jeff's strained expression. "Buck up. Your wife is the one who's going to do all the work."

"Not without me, she isn't," Jeff replied. He tied the green cloth face mask over his lips. "How do I look?"

"Great. But wait a moment. We had a fax message for you. It's marked Urgent."

"Read it to me while we walk to my wife's room," he answered. "And it had better be good."

"Sounds like it." The nurse held the facsimile in front of her and as they walked, she read.

"Dear Jeff,

"I want you to know I've had time to think about what I told you and Abby. I was wrong and I'm sorry. Too bad it had to take my illness to make me see the light.

"I want you to know there's nothing more important than children, and that means you and Elaine. I knew that, even though I may not have shown it. Now that I realize how much you and Abby love each other, I wish you both the best of everything. In your writing, too. If you can see your way clear to help out with the Logan Wilshire for a while, I'd appreciate it.

"Your mother and Elaine send their love. Take good care of my grandson.

                                    "Love, Dad."

By the time the woman was finished reading, tears were in Jeff's eyes.

"Wow, that's some message," the nurse murmured. "I'll bet it makes you happy."

"You can say that again," Jeff agreed. "Happier than you know."

"Is the baby a boy?"

Jeff shrugged. "My wife and I have never bothered to find out, but we named him Patrick, just the same. We'll be just as happy if she turns out to be a girl. Thank you." He pushed open the door to Abby's room with an elbow.

"It's about time," Dr. Beth Gardner commented. "I was afraid you were going to miss the birth of your baby."

"Never," Jeff replied. "Not after all I went through to become a father."

The attendants in the room started to laugh. Even Abby, trying hard to breathe properly, had to giggle.

"That's not what I meant," Jeff corrected. "I only meant that I had to be a father in training before I could convince Abby that I could be a good father."

Abby squeezed his hand. "He even earned a diploma." Then she bore down and grunted as she strained to deliver the baby.

"Well, that's a first," her doctor said. "And here's another one. Your first son!"

With a final flurry, little Patrick Logan made his appearance.

Jeff gazed in wonder at the baby that the doctor laid on Abby's breast. He counted ten tiny red toes, ten tiny red fingers, and a rosebud mouth that was already at work letting the world know he'd arrived.

The doctor took pity on Jeff. "Want to hold Patrick for a minute while we finish up here?"

Jeff gingerly reached for his son and cuddled him

in his arms. "Hello, fella. This is your dad speaking.
We're going to get real acquainted later," he whispered, "but I want to tell you now that I've loved
you and your mother for a long, long time. And that
I intend to be the best father ever."

Abby gazed at her husband and son with all the
love in her. Jeff held her heart and her future in his
hands. With him, she knew she'd be cared for,
watched over. There would be no more lonely days
and nights. Instead, the days would be filled with
excitement and the adventure of discovering the
world through Jeff's eyes. There would be nights of
Jeff holding her, making love with her. And now,
Patrick to love.

"Say," Jeff told Abby as he handed back their
son, "I just remembered there's going to be Kate
and Sebastian's twins to add to the family. I'll bet
Patrick is going to make a great brother. Or is he a
cousin?"

Abby nodded happily. "Both."

Jeff studied the squirming baby. "You don't suppose there's a school for prospective grandfathers,
do you?"

"Not again!" Abby responded. "By the time the
twins are born, I guarantee you'll know all there is
to know about babies. You know," she went on, "I
checked Patrick's horoscope a while back. He's a
Scorpio—warm, loving, intelligent and imaginative.
Just like his father."

COMING NEXT MONTH

#777 SURPRISE—YOU'RE A DADDY! by Judy Christenberry
4 Tots for 4 Texans
Spence Hauk never forgot that night when he made love to Melanie Rule.
She was everything he'd wanted, even though she was in love with another
man. But now that Melanie is carrying his child, the rugged cowboy wants
his family—baby *and* wife.

#778 COWBOY IN A TUX by Mary Anne Wilson
Delaney's Grooms
Cowboy J. T. Watson disliked weddings—some years ago he'd been the
groom in one that lasted one night. But this cowboy's on a run of bad
luck when his ex, Candice, ends up his partner at his friend's nuptials...
and he finds a message in his tux that says, "You're still married!"

#779 DIAMOND DADDIES by Linda Cajio
Every man's greatest fortune is his family. Only, twin brothers and
confirmed bachelors Jeff and Julian Diamond don't know it yet. So their
matchmaking grandfather is determined to make sure they have incentive
to marry and give him grandbabies—plus a hefty tax break—by the end
of the year.

#780 STUD FOR HIRE? by Debbi Rawlins
When a stranger tried to hire Adam Knight to romance her "poor,
heartbroken" friend, Adam said "No way!" But the next thing he knew,
"poor" Gracie Allen had stolen his heart. Would she ever believe it when
she learned his secret?

Look us up on-line at: http://www.romance.net